I0733808

ISBN 978-1-957909-01-1



Cover art by Leslie Reilly

This is primarily a work of fiction. Depictions of historical events and people are rooted in fact, although certain characters, characterizations, incidents, locations, and dialogue have been fictionalized or invented for proposes of dramatization.

# Acknowledgements

Little stories parallel big stories. Although Meg couldn't influence the incarceration of Japanese-Americans in concentration camps,  or the development of the atomic bomb, it's interesting to think of these world-shaking events happening at the same time as Meg's individual quest for friendship and belonging.

Perhaps the lessons Meg learned about courage and loyalty were the same lessons learned by World War II scientists and warriors, if we're lucky. After all, they were all human.

Thank you to the Manzanar National Historic Site park rangers, especially Dr. Patricia Biggs, who found a photo of my grandfather taken outside the Manzanar barrack that once housed the Protestant church. This is one story of many families affected by Executive Order 9066. It is also a story for third culture children who have to figure out whether they belong to the country on their passport or the country where their parents work. Sometimes it's hard to figure out whether both places, or neither, is home.

When it comes down to it, home is where the rocks are. Home is where the water flows. Home is where the art is. Meg and her family owe a great debt to photographer Ansel Adams, who used his lens to show them the beauty around them, both inside and outside the camp.

I hope you enjoy this book.


Katy Hammel

Before anything were the rocks.

# Chapter 1
# A Rocky Beginning

*Meg*

Meg Binnenkerk sat on the back stoop of her Grandmother's house in the winter of 1942, looking out at the snow draped over the dead garden. The snow glistened silver and white as far as Meg could see, except on the narrow walkway that wrapped around to the front of the house.

It was a peaceful enough scene, except for one small problem. A rock had somehow worked its way inside her winter boot. The boots were too small to begin with. They were hand-me-downs from the church, thin and rubbery, more like rain galoshes than snow boots. Meg would have to peel the boot off her foot to dig for the pebble.

She could have gone inside, taken off both boots, and abandoned the idea of being outside altogether. It would be warm inside, but no doubt baby Amy would be fussing, Mother would be resting, and Grandmother would press Meg into some chore. Meg would rather strip to her bare feet outside, no matter how cold it was.

Meg finally took her boot and sock off because the pebble — it was a tiny thing — was inside her sock. How did it get there? With a sigh, Meg turned the sock inside out, feeling for any more pebbles, then rolled the sock back on her foot. She took off the other boot, too, and checked for pebbles, then pulled them back on. The boots made a slurpy sound as they stretched over her damp socks.

Sitting on the stone stoop allowed the winter cold to creep through Meg's plaid wool pants and into the backs of her thighs. Meg told herself she should stand up soon, before her whole body turned numb. Maybe she should walk over to her uncles' house. Her younger brother Walter would be there, working on engines and talking about cars with their uncles. Walter was crazy for cars and engines, but they didn't interest Meg. Meg hadn't found much to do in small town Zeeland, Michigan.

Meg held the tiny pebble in her hand. The pebble was her only little bit of company there in the silent backyard. Meg contemplated throwing the pebble as hard as she could into the garden, where it could settle under the snow amidst the broken stalks of corn plants and the shriveled watermelon vine. But if this pebble wanted to stay with her, that was okay, too. Meg dropped the pebble into her coat pocket.

## *The Rocks*

Far from Michigan, buried in the heart of Africa, in the land called the Congo, were the most powerful rocks in the world. Formed over millennia through a confluence of unique geological happenstances, these rocks were distinct from other rocks in the world and very different from the pebble in Meg's pocket. These rocks were ribboned with rare Earth elements like radium and uranium.

Potters and chemists found interesting things to do with these minerals. Among other things, when the radium was crushed into a powder and mixed with water, it made a paint that glowed in the dark.

Over in America, companies hired young ladies to paint glow-in-the-dark numbers on the faces of clocks and watches. That way, customers could see the time even in the middle of the night. These employees would wet thin brushes in water, dip them in the radium powder, curl the tip of the bristles into a point using their teeth or lips, and then carefully paint the cursive numbers. Over and over. Wet, dip, curl, paint.

The young women thought they had good jobs. The work was creative, precise, and well-paid. Little did they know the radium paint was poison.

The rare Earth elements like radium and uranium are radioactive. The nuclei of each atom is packed with tiny particles buzzing and colliding as if trying to escape.

The same subatomic particles that made radium glow in the dark made it very dangerous to human bones and organs.

Over time, the clock painters swallowed so much radium that their bodies glowed in the dark. Then their bones collapsed. They grew unable to walk. One by one, they died.

Instead of cursing the rocks, instead of returning them to the ground, people found other ways to use these rocks.

By 1938, the interest in the rocks had become more than ornamental. The Germans wanted the rocks. It wasn't that the Germans wanted to paint numbers on clocks. Oh no. A German chemist named Dr. Otto Hahn noticed that when he mixed radium with other chemicals, the concoction would release a stream of invisible neutron particles. When Dr. Hahn positioned the neutrons to flow over uranium, with a buffer of wax in between to slow the neutrons down, the uranium would swallow a few of the loose neutrons. When that happened, the atoms of uranium would get too full, too unstable, and burst open.

What Dr. Hahn found especially curious was how the uranium changed when it burst. His chemical tests showed that when the uranium atoms burst, they broke into elements lower down on the periodic table, like barium. His German colleague Dr. Ida Noddack had reported the same thing four years earlier, but Dr. Hahn had rejected her reports as "really absurd." He didn't believe the uranium had actually transformed. Until he saw it himself.

# Chapter Two
# Getting Out

## *Meg*

Most missionary families got out of Japan well before the war began, but Father had been ordered by the Japanese to stay behind. He eventually got a berth out on a freighter in December of 1941; they knew that much from his last letter. But the Japanese attacked Pearl Harbor while the ship was at sea and the freighter turned right back around.

Now Meg's two favorite countries were at war, her father was being kept prisoner in Japan, and some of the meaner boys at school called Meg and Walter "dirty, yellow Japs." Meg and Walter weren't Japanese. They had just lived in Japan while their parents worked there.

They weren't dirty or yellow, either, but when had bullies ever made sense?

Meg had truly tried her best to make friends in Zeeland. She even went to Violet's birthday party, but that had been a disaster. Meg shuddered and sat back down on the cold stone stoop. She decided she would think back through every moment of the party to purge the shame of it and banish it from her memory.

She remembered putting on her best dress. She remembered looking into the mirror to straighten out her hair bow, reminding herself firmly to speak only English at the party. Grandmother had walked her over to Violet's house. Meg had walked in the house empty-handed without any present to give the birthday girl.

Violet's mother had welcomed her in a little too heartily and spoke to her a little too loudly, as if she was a foreigner who didn't speak English. It was clear to Meg that the only reason she had been invited in the first place was that Meg's grandmother and Violet's grandmother were lifelong friends.

Meg had walked past the gift table in the foyer and sat down on the long davenport in the living room. Violet's father was about to start a game. He slid an LP out of its cover, making a big show of hiding the cover from the party goers. He placed the record gently on the record player and positioned the needle carefully somewhere in the middle of a song. The music started. Whoever yelled out the title of the song first was the winner. Then the girls cheered and started singing along.

Meg didn't recognize the first song, nor the second, nor any of them. She was too new to the U.S. She didn't know any American pop songs. She couldn't even pretend she was just about to get the title of the song. It was on the tip of her tongue! No, it wasn't.

Pretending to sing along would have been worse than waiting silently for the game to end. As Meg sat stiffly, her discomfort turned into anger. Violet had her father with her, leading a silly game at a children's party. Meg didn't have her father, and even if she did, he wouldn't have participated in such a frivolous activity. Not that the Binnenkerks even owned a record player. They had been lucky their house in Japan had electricity. Most Japanese homes in the 1930's and 40's didn't.

Meg could feel the other girls looking at her, scorning her for her ignorance. Finally, Violet's father ended the game and the girls turned their loud attention to the gift table. Violet unwrapped a lipstick, a magazine with actress Deena Durban on the cover, and a pair of stockings with an actual seam up the back. It was just the perfect shade, just the perfect movie star, just the right things for a teenager in America.

But Meg didn't care one whit about lipstick or movie stars or stockings. She had nothing in common with these girls, except nationality.

Meg stirred herself for a brave attempt to be socially appropriate. She stood up and found Violet's mother in the kitchen, asking politely if she could help.

"Of course you may!" Violet's mother leaned in to that idea and chatted away merrily, giving Meg the napkins and forks to carry to the table. Meg set the table with napkins and forks, sat at the large table with the other girls, sang Happy Birthday - finally a song she knew - and ate a slice of the cake. Never had Meg been so grateful to see Walter when he appeared at Violet's door to accompany Meg back to Grandmother's. Meg was sure Violet was grateful for her departure, too. Violet's party could swing merrily on without an awkward stranger standing like a stork in the middle of a flock of flamingos.

Ticking back through the memories of that party hadn't helped erase the embarrassment at all. The truth was that Meg had only the slightest idea how to be American, and no desire to flounce around like the girls at the party. Meg picked up a cold stick from the stoop and starting tracing shapes in the snow.

## *The Rocks*

Dr. Hahn's laboratory in Germany was supposed to be a place for the peaceful pursuit of knowledge, but the same could not be said for the rest of Europe. As the Nazis gained power, they made life miserable for everyone around them, especially Jewish families. It got the point where even the most esteemed scientists in Germany and Italy and Hungary and Poland, if they were part or all Jewish, or were married to Jewish spouses, were forced to flee for their lives.

Dr. Hahn's long-time research partner, Dr. Lise Meitner, was one of these émigré scientists. Dr. Hahn helped her escape from Germany to Sweden. Then he continued their experiments using the equipment and instruments she left behind. They wrote letters back and forth to continue to work together as best they could. It was no surprise, then, that Dr. Meitner was the first person to hear about the odd thing Dr. Hahn noticed in the uranium experiments.

Over the Christmas holiday late in 1938, Dr. Meitner and her nephew, the young researcher Dr. Otto Frisch, pondered what the observations meant. They did some mathematical calculations on the mass of the uranium before and after the split. Their computations proved that the uranium atom was indeed splitting into two medium-sized parts, like a droplet of water that gets too big and separates into two droplets. Except two droplets of water are still water, while the uranium was fragmenting into different elements altogether. Dr. Meitner understood what was happening was truly "fission" of the uranium atoms.

Interestingly, the math showed that the chunks didn't quite add up to the mass of the original uranium. Something was lost along the way. Dr. Meitner realized the little bit of mass lost in this transaction had converted to energy. It was just as Dr. Albert Einstein had theorized in his famous equation: mass and energy could be interchangeable. Every time a uranium atom split open, it released a little pop of energy.

The Germans weren't the only scientists using neutrons to trigger changes in various elements. Ever since the famous British scientist Dr. James Chadwick had proven the existence of neutrons, scientists in laboratories around the world were using neutrons to poke at other elements to see what would happen. They thought they might be able to produce some useful variations of the materials, like isotopes of radium that could cure, rather than cause, disease. But what Dr. Noddack and Dr. Hahn observed was different. They weren't seeing slight modifications of uranium; they were seeing uranium actually break open and release more neutrons along the way.

Over in Poland, physicist Dr. Joseph Rotblat was wondering what happened to the neutrons that escaped when heavy atoms split open. He started looking at the way the neutrons scattered when uranium broke apart.

Hungarian expert Dr. Leo Szilárd already had a theory about this. He thought, if the split of an atom set a neutron free, that loose neutron might trigger another atom to split, and that split might free another neutron, in an ongoing, self-sustaining cycle. In other words, one initial fission in a tiny bit of uranium might set off a chain reaction.

That led the scientists to the next thought. What if an element like uranium released more than one neutron when it split? Then each of those neutrons could split another atom of uranium and each of those freed neutrons could split some more. The fission reaction could expand exponentially.

Dr. Meitner's nephew Dr. Frisch had calculated that the split of one atom of uranium released enough energy to make a single grain of sand hop. That may not sound like a lot. But if a single atom splitting could make a grain of sand hop, what would trillions and trillions of atoms do if they exploded in an exponentially-growing chain reaction? That would generate a truly spectacular wallop of energy. In other words, it could be a bomb.

After his holiday with his aunt, Dr. Frisch shared his calculations with Denmark's preeminent physicist Dr. Niels Bohr, who announced the discovery just days later at a conference in Washington, D.C. Within a week, American physicist Dr. Robert Oppenheimer sketched a diagram on his chalkboard showing how a nuclear bomb might work.

The news had gotten out.

# Chapter 3
# Waiting and Watching

## *Meg*

Meg's father was home. He looked different: gaunt, sick, and coughing. But it was his coat, his smile, his thin mustache. The Swedish Red Cross had negotiated a deal for Meg's father and other western prisoners to be traded for Japanese nationals living in the U.S. Lots of people had gotten stuck where they didn't belong when war broke out. Only a neutral country like Sweden could negotiate people trades among enemy nations. And it worked. It had been a harrowing journey for Father through mine-infested waters, but finally, he was home.

Except that Father didn't fit at Grandmother's house. Whenever Walter absented himself - which was most of the time - Grandmother's house was filled entirely with women. Grandmother ruled the roost. Baby Amy screamed. Mother hid in her bed.

Meg sat warily and watched. In Meg's opinion, now that Father was here, it was time for the Binnenkerks to get out of Zeeland.

Meg let her mind drift back to the summers her family had spent at Lake Nojiri in Japan. That's where all the missionary families gathered for summer vacation. Each family had a wooden cabin on the slope of a hill. It was 185 steps from the bottom of the hill up to the Binnenkerks' cabin. Along the way back up the hill after swimming in the lake, they would stop at the pump to fill a jug of water for drinking and washing.

Meg had eaten her very first hot dog at Lake Nojiri. She remembered the ketchup dripping out the end of the bun. She remembered how the wooden boathouse smelled like mustard from lifejackets that had gotten wet and dried off a hundred times. She remembered long carved wooden oars hung on pegs above the sliding boathouse doors.

Hanako and the other Japanese housekeepers came with them to Lake Nojiri. They got a vacation, too. The ministers took turns preaching and then everyone played tennis and ate ice cream cones. Mother and Father played couples tennis, exchanging a joke and a smile and then getting into position for the next serve.

After the game, win or lose, they would jog in tandem to the net and shake hands with their opponents.

Could they get there again? If they couldn't get back to Lake Nojiri, could they at least get back to being the family they used to be?

## *The Rocks*

A bomb fueled by nuclear fission? That was a tantalizing, terrifying idea.

There appeared to be three ingredients needed for this bomb recipe: first, some kind of initiator like the radium mixture to start off a flow of neutrons; second, a moderator like wax to slow the neutrons down and keep them from bouncing off the fissile material; and third, the purest, most fissionable uranium in the world.

That's what made those rocks from the Congo the most important rocks in the world. They contained uranium in the highest concentrations human beings had ever seen. To be sure, there were uranium deposits underground in other parts of the world, including under Navajo Nation land in the American Southwest. But those rocks from the heart of Africa? They were the most freakishly uranium-rich rocks in the world. Of course the Nazis wanted them. Everyone who knew anything about the news pinging back and forth between the scientists wanted to get their hands on those rocks.

The rocks were in Africa, but they weren't owned by Africans. The European country of Belgium had conquered and colonized the Congo. A Belgian company ran the Shinkolobwe mining operation that used Congolese workers to dig these rocks from the ground. Then the Belgian company sold the rocks and pocketed the profits.

Looking back at it now, it's no exaggeration to say that the person who ran that Belgian company, which controlled that mine, which dug up those rocks, was perhaps the most important person in the world.

His name was Edgar Sengier.

In May of 1939, Mr. Sengier was in London making deals for the various minerals his company controlled. The Congo had lots of rocks to offer, not just radium-uranium ore. It was during that trip that Mr. Sengier met with Sir Henry Tizard from England's Imperial College of Science and Technology.

Sir Henry nodded to the dapper Belgian gentlemen and got right to the point. The British government wanted to buy all the radium-uranium ore extracted from the Shinkolobwe mine. England would control the future of this research.

Mr. Sengier said no.

Sir Henry took Mr. Sengier by the arm and warned him to be careful. Sir Henry pointed out that Mr. Sengier had in his hands something that may mean a catastrophe to both of their countries if the rocks were ever to fall in the hands of a possible enemy.

Mr. Sengier knew what Sir Henry meant. His country, Belgium, shared a border with Germany. If the Nazis invaded Belgium, took the rocks, and figured out how to make the world's first atomic bomb, they would be unstoppable.

Even so, Mr. Sengier shook his head. He did not choose England to steward these rocks.

France asked for the rocks, too. This request came from Dr. Irène Joliot-Curie, the daughter of the famous radium scientist Dr. Marie Curie.

Dr. Joliot-Curie proposed that France and Belgium work together to develop a fission bomb, in a secret laboratory in the Saharan Desert on the African continent. Perhaps including Belgium in the plan would make the deal more attractive to Mr. Sengier.

Mr. Sengier agreed to provide Dr. Joliot-Curie with enough uranium to conduct her experiments.

But not all of the rocks. Not the entire stockpile.

Across the Atlantic Ocean, the United States of America had become the second home for many uprooted scientists, including Dr. Szilárd from Hungary, and of course, the most famous of them all, Dr. Albert Einstein, who, as it turned out, was friends with the Queen of Belgium. Dr. Szilárd and a couple of other scientists drove out to Dr. Einstein's house on Long Island to talk with him about the Congolese rocks.

Dr. Szilárd pressed Dr. Einstein to write to the Queen of Belgium. He wanted Dr. Einstein to urge her to get the Shinkolobwe rocks out of Belgium before Germany could invade. Ever prepared, Dr. Szilárd had already drafted the letter he wanted Dr. Einstein to sign.

But Dr. Einstein decided not to write to the Queen of Belgium. Instead, he wrote to the President of the United States. The U.S. was his home now, and Dr. Einstein believed his first duty was to alert President Franklin Delano Roosevelt.

In the letter, Dr. Einstein told President Roosevelt that "it may become possible to set up a nuclear chain reaction in a large mass of uranium, by which vast amounts of power and large quantities of new radium-like elements would be generated."

Dr. Einstein went on. "[I]t is conceivable — though much less certain — that extremely powerful bombs of a new type may thus be constructed."

If an atomic bomb fueled by uranium was possible, where would the uranium come from? Dr. Einstein told President Roosevelt that too: "The most important source of uranium is Belgian Congo."

President Roosevelt wrote back, saying he would look into it.

Then the Nazis invaded Poland.

Fortunately, Dr. Joseph Rotblat had gotten out of Poland in time. He'd made it to England and took a job in Dr. Chadwick's laboratory. Sadly, his wife had been too sick to travel. She had to be left behind. Now, she was trapped in Poland.

Everyone knew the Nazis wouldn't stop with Poland. All of the countries bordering Germany - Belgium, France, Denmark and Holland - were in danger of Nazi invasion. Mr. Sengier could foresee that when the Nazis got to Belgium, they would certainly take over his company. They would seize his uranium. And if they got as far as Africa, they would take over the Shinkolobwe mine and dig out even more uranium rocks.

Mr. Sengier did what he could. He ordered a halt to the mining. He ordered the Congolese to flood the Shinkolobwe mine with water. If the Nazis got that far, they would find the mine inoperable. At least, it would slow them down.

Of course, tons of uranium ore had already been tunneled out of the ground and piled up around the mine entrance. Those rocks had to escape Hitler, too. They needed to be loaded onto trains, carted to the coast of Africa, and then transported onto ships to steam away.

The ships could travel up the coast to Portugal, but they couldn't stay there, nor in France, nor Belgium, nor anywhere along the European continent. Mr. Sengier realized that these rocks, and his entire company, had to cross the Atlantic Ocean. They had to get to America.

Mr. Sengier moved to New York City and leased space for his company headquarters in the fancy Cunard Building on Manhattan island. Then he rented warehouse space close by. As each shipment of uranium ore crossed the Atlantic Ocean and arrived in New York harbor, it was unloaded and piled high in the warehouses.

Shipload after shipload, twelve hundred tons of uranium ore made it safely across the Atlantic Ocean and into the rented Baker & Williams warehouses in New York City.

There it sat for nearly three years, while the Binnenkerks spent their last happy summers at Lake Nojiri, while the clock of history ticked toward war.

# Chapter 4
# Attempts at Communication

## *Meg*

Even if she didn't have a single friend in Zeeland, Michigan, Meg could be a good big sister. Right now, that meant introducing Amy to Father, slowly, very slowly. Father may have dreamed about his new baby being born, but Amy didn't know him at all, and the introductions had to be made at Amy's pace.

If Father picked her up, Amy screamed and reached out for Meg. Meg felt cross, more with Father than with Amy. Meg would never have scolded her father, of course, but she felt like it. Father should have known better. It wasn't as though time stood still while he was imprisoned. It seemed that just getting Father back didn't automatically make everything all right.

## *The Rocks*

The world was far from all right. Every day from his office in the Cunard Building in downtown Manhattan, Mr. Sengier unfolded the newspaper and read about the war. After conquering Poland, the Nazis headed north and invaded Denmark and Norway. Then they swung to the west. Belgium and Holland fell in a German blitzkrieg, the Nazis' "lightning war." Mr. Sengier's beloved homeland was now in enemy hands.

France was the Nazis' next conquest. That put an abrupt end to Mr. Sengier's plan to conduct uranium experiments with Dr. Irène Joliot-Curie.

Then England came under attack from German planes, submarines and spies. There were night-time raids. A blitz over London. England was holding its ground, but not without bitter fighting. Italy's Prime Minister, Benito Mussolini, sided with the Nazis. Within a year, the Axis powers had invaded Yugoslavia and mainland Greece, then the island of Crete in the Mediterranean Sea. Then the Nazis assaulted Russia to the northeast. They also spread south, crossing the rest of the Mediterranean Sea and over to North Africa. The fight had reached the continent of Africa. The Nazis weren't in central Africa yet, not in the Congo, but the fighting in the north was especially fierce.

American factories retooled and geared up. Now they worked day and night to manufacture weapons, fighter planes, and ships. The U.S. needed all the supplies it could get to fight off the threats from Germany in Europe and Japan in Asia.

That meant Mr. Sengier's company had a new customer.

What did the U.S. want to buy from Mr. Sengier's Belgian company? "Cobalt," the U.S. State Department said to Mr. Sengier in March of 1942. Would Mr. Sengier please double the production of cobalt coming out of the Katanga mines in the African Congo?

Cobalt from Katanga? That's what the U.S. wanted?

The Americans needed cobalt to make stronger metal alloys for ships and planes.

Mr. Sengier agreed to sell cobalt to the Americans. In the back of his mind, though, he thought about the radium-uranium rocks from the Shinkolobwe mine. Why weren't the Americans asking him for those rocks?

Mr. Sengier had reached a decision about who should get his precious uranium rocks. He wrote to the U.S. war department, offering to sell the Americans the radium-uranium ore from the Shinkolobwe mine. But no one wrote back.

After a couple of weeks, he wrote again. This time, he was even more blunt. He wrote: "these ores containing radium and uranium are very valuable."

Of course, other than a small number of nuclear physicists and chemists around the world, very few people knew why these rocks were so valuable. Mr. Sengier's second letter went unanswered, too.

# Chapter 5
# A New Mission

*Meg*

It was a fine fall day in New York City in September of 1942. This was the day Reverend Howard Binnenkerk was finally going to learn his new assignment. His cough was still a problem. His lungs hurt every day. But he had rested and recovered as best he could. He was ready to get back to work.

What use was a Christian missionary, though, while Japan was closed to westerners? Through his long months of captivity, Howard Binnenkerk used his language skills to translate between the Japanese guards and their prisoners. He'd tried to encourage the Japanese guards to be gentle. He'd tried to model Christian virtue. He'd tried to convince himself that his imprisonment was only a temporary detour in his mission work, but it was hard to shake the feeling that the war had eroded whatever progress missionaries had made in Japan.

It hadn't been easy to introduce Christianity to Japan. Missionaries were welcome to set up orphanages and hospitals and schools, but most Japanese had other faiths. Howard had even met the Japanese Emperor on occasion. It was hard to reconcile the the serene Shinto devotee he'd met at the palace in Tokyo with the ruthless imperialist who had no qualms about invading China and attacking the U.S. It was hard to fathom that same man was now ordering suicidal kamikaze attacks on American troops.

The Japanese guards were convinced that Japan was winning every battle, but Howard had suspected that wasn't true. Now that he was back in the U.S., he realized he had been right to be doubtful. The war was going much worse for Japan than their people had been led to believe.

Even his own family had changed so much. Amy hadn't even been born when he'd sent the family out of Japan. She was an adorable blonde bundle now, but she didn't even know him. She still screamed when he tried to pick her up.

Meg and Walter seemed so much older, taller, more distant. They listened to him, but they tended to take their cues from each other rather than from him. They had a way of looking at each other, silently making decisions that circumvented him.

As glad as he was to be free, Howard was restless to get back to Japan. Being a missionary was his life's calling, his understanding of what God wanted him to do. How long would it be before he could get back there, and what shape would Japan be in?

His meeting with the Mission Board was scheduled for later in the afternoon, a few blocks up Broadway at Trinity Church, but, for now, Howard Binnenkerk sat on the steps of the Cunard Building and occupied himself with people-watching. The sun beamed down on the steps. Howard appreciated its warmth. Across Broadway, he could see the cobblestone sidewalk around a triangular park. Around him, busy New Yorkers moved with purpose, well-dressed and accessorized, seemingly without a care in the world. They weren't gazing warily at the sky, dreading an aerial attack, ears tuned for an air raid siren. They weren't in fear of beatings or torture. They had plenty of food, blankets to sleep in, and freedom to move about as they liked.

Howard watched an elegant European gentleman mount the steps of the Cunard building. He was older, white-haired, wearing a double-breasted suit that looked more like a tuxedo than a business suit. The suit was a soft black with perfect creases along the pant legs. A dainty wedge of silk poked out the top of his chest pocket. The man disappeared through the revolving doors into the building.

Next came a taller man, striding with purpose. Howard suspected he was a military man, even though he wasn't in uniform. There was something in his stride, his posture, and his shoes that gave it away.

This man was carrying a briefcase. That was the difference, Howard thought. The people who belonged to the building had no need to carry a case, because their important papers were already inside being handled by aides. Men like that had cases that were shepherded from personal valets to drivers to secretaries. This military man was a visitor, here to do business in the Cunard Building.

## *The Rocks*

Father was right. Colonel Nichols was a military man, although he purposefully wore civilian clothes that day in September of 1942 when he walked into the Cunard Building. He was there for one very specific purpose. Mr. Sengier's letters had finally reached the people in the know. Colonel Nichols was dispatched by the U.S. Army to make a deal with Mr. Sengier to buy the Belgian uranium. The trick was that he had to close the deal without alerting Mr. Sengier why the U.S. wanted it. Under no circumstances was Colonel Nichols allowed to disclose the secret; President Roosevelt had given the order to develop a nuclear bomb.

Another Army man, Colonel Groves, was appointed to run the project. Almost immediately, he was promoted to General. General Groves would need that title and level of authority to implement such an audacious plan. Developing this bomb would require a large laboratory, a network of factories to make whatever equipment and material were needed, and experts of all kinds - chemists and physicists, metallurgists, engineers, mathematicians, and technicians, all of them sworn to the utmost secrecy. Of course, nothing could begin without uranium. The whole plan hinged on Colonel Nichols making this deal with Mr. Sengier of the Belgian mining company.

Colonel Nichols opened his wallet and showed Mr. Sengier his Army ID. That's when it dawned on Mr. Sengier that this visit might be different than his other dealings with civilian purchasing agents.

"I understand that you have some uranium to sell?" Colonel Nichols asked.

Well, well, Mr. Sengier thought. The Americans weren't asking for cobalt this time. "Are you a contracting officer?" Mr. Sengier asked bluntly. "Do you have authority to buy?"

Colonel Nichols looked directly into Mr. Sengier's face. "I have more authority, I'm sure, than you have uranium to sell." Colonel Nichols fell silent. Had he gone too far? What he had said was no less than the truth. The U.S. would buy all the uranium Mr. Sengier had to sell and still want more. If there was any chance a bomb would work, the U.S. would want to control all the uranium on the planet. But the colonel hadn't meant to sound flippant. He definitely didn't want to offend Mr. Sengier, who was no doubt used to more decorous business dealings.

Mr. Sengier took a breath. He wondered if Colonel Nichols knew what he was asking for. Finally, he asked, "Will the uranium ore be used for military purposes?" Mr. Sengier definitely did not want to hear that these precious rocks would be used to paint glow-in-the-dark dials on airplanes, or to make stronger metal alloys. The future of his beloved Belgium and the whole of Europe rested on unleashing the inner power of those rocks. Did this American know what he was asking for?

Colonel Nichols hesitated. Only a few people in America knew that President Roosevelt had given the order to develop a bomb. It was the most secret of secrets in the war. Mr. Sengier wasn't in the Army. He wasn't even American. There was no way he could be included in the secret.

Mr. Sengier watched Colonel Nichols weigh his next words. Mr. Sengier realized the pause alone told him what he wanted to know. Mr. Sengier found a way for Colonel Nichols to save face. "All I want is your assurance as an Army officer that this uranium ore is definitely going to be used for war purposes."

"Yes," Colonel Nichols said. That much he could say without equivocation.

"Then let's make a deal, Colonel," Mr. Sengier said briskly. "My company, the Union Minière, has twelve hundred tons of uranium available."

More than a thousand tons? Colonel Nichols could feel his heart thumping.

Mr. Sengier kept going, his voice matter-of-fact. "When do you need it?"

"If it wasn't impossible, I'd say tomorrow."

"It's not impossible. You can have immediately one thousand tons of uranium ore."

"Immediately? Where are these rocks?" Colonel Nichols asked.

Mr. Sengier waved his hand in the direction of Staten Island. Then he pulled out a pad of paper. The two men reached a contract in just a few sentences for the transfer of ownership of the entire stockpile of uranium ore held by Union Minière in the New York warehouses.

They barely haggled over the price. Mr. Sengier wasn't after more riches. He wanted Belgium back. He had chosen his hero in the race for a nuclear bomb.

Payments would be made to a hidden bank account. Government auditors would be instructed to look the other way. A few sentences and a handshake and Mr. Sengier's company had a deal with the United States of America.

Twelve hundred tons of uranium ore sounded like plenty to make a bomb. Even so, Colonel Nichols wasn't quite done. "Is there uranium still at the mine in Africa?" he asked Mr. Sengier.

Yes. Mr. Sengier had to admit there was still about three thousand tons on the ground outside the mine.

Colonel Nichols said, "The U.S. will buy it all. Can it all be shipped here in the next three weeks?"

Mr. Sengier suggested it would be better to move the ore a little at a time, in smaller quantities on faster ships that could outrun the German U-boats. After all, the seas were far more treacherous than they had been in 1939.

Colonel Nichols agreed. What about uranium still underground?

Mr. Sengier explained that he had flooded the mine.

The U.S. would purchase the mining rights from Belgium, pump out the water, and dig out every uranium rock. There was no doubt the U.S. would strive to acquire all the uranium in the world. Because these rocks weren't just tactical advantage in the war. They weren't just political power between countries. If a bomb became reality, these African rocks would steer the fate of the planet.

This was one of those moments, rare in the history of the world, when two people conceive a plan that stretches across oceans, continents, countries, and generations.

But there was an even harder question for Colonel Nichols to ask. He had to find out if there was Shinkolobwe ore in Belgium when the Nazis took over.

Mr. Sengier admitted that, despite his best efforts, there had been a shipment on the docks when the Nazis invaded.

Of course, the Nazis already had some uranium ore in the laboratory where Dr. Meitner and Dr. Hahn worked. Paris was also under German occupation, which meant the Nazis controlled Dr. Irène Joliot-Curie's laboratory and the supply of uranium she was using there. And there was a uranium of lesser quality in a mine in Czechoslovakia, another country under Nazi dominion. Even so, hearing that an entire shipload of Shinkolobwe uranium was lost to enemy hands was deeply concerning.

Mr. Sengier and Colonel Nichols looked at one another. The Nazis had uranium and now the Americans had uranium. It was going to be a race to see who could figure out first how to use it to make a bomb.

The Nazis had a head start. They had Dr. Hahn, for one thing. He was still working away in his laboratory, as was another famous German scientist, Dr. Werner Heisenberg. But now the U.S. had the grand prize: an unspeakably valuable treasure trove of dusty yellowish rocks hiding in plain sight in New York City.

# Chapter 6
# Ready, Set, Go

*Meg*

Meg looked out the train window and watched the electrical line swoop up and down. The power line was just a thin gray wire linked from pole to pole, rising up to kiss the top of the pole, then swooping down and up again to the next pole. As the train sped by, the swooping of the power line created a rhythm like waves. Had the wire been stretched tight when it was first connected? Did it sag over time, or was it designed to have a little slack? Meg wondered what it was like to be an electrical worker, unspooling the cable, climbing up the ladder to connect it, then down and over to the next pole, again and again for mile after mile.

Meg and her family were traveling west on the Santa Fe Chief train. All of Meg's clothes fit in a valise tucked on the rack above their seats. Walter had shared the seat with her, but now he was off somewhere exploring the train. Mother, Father, and Amy sat on the other side of the aisle. Mother had dressed for the trip, wearing red lipstick and her smartest suit topped with her best hat. Now she was asleep, slumped against the train window with Amy napping in her lap.

Father was taking them to Independence, California, where he had been assigned to work as a chaplain in a prison camp. The camp held American families, ordinary in every respect but one: they were Japanese-Americans who had been living along the west coast of California.

When Japan attacked Pearl Harbor, the U.S. government rounded up the leading businessmen, priests, and community leaders in Japanese-American neighborhoods along the West Coast, suspecting they might be spies for the enemy. Then the government ordered all their families to join the exodus, too, packing up their belonging and trading their homes for makeshift shacks in prison camps.

How ironic that this camp where the Japanese-American families were being held captive was right next to a town called Independence.

At least the prisoners would have a pastor who was fluent in Japanese. Many of the older Japanese-

Americans were issei, first generation Americans born in Japan. Even some of the nisei, second generation Americans, used Japanese as their primary language.

Meg had no regrets about leaving Zeeland behind. As far as she was concerned, the farther west the Santa Fe Chief could carry them, the better.

The uncles had driven them to the train station in New Holland, Michigan, where they boarded the local for the ride into Chicago. That's where the Santa Fe Chief began its grand cross-county journey.

Meg thought the train station in Chicago looked like a cathedral: a giant space with an elegant arched ceiling. Now Meg wondered if the arc of that ceiling matched the swoop of the electrical lines outside the train. Was there a common angle or arc that was especially pleasing to the eye, whether it was in a roof arching up or a power line sagging down? The ceiling of the train station seemed designed to proclaim that it was defying gravity, while the power lines succumbed to it.

I need to learn how to measure curves, Meg thought.

Walter would probably tease her, telling her the curve of the swoop depended entirely on how close the poles were to each other and how tightly the electrical line had been fed between the poles. Walter would look so serious giving his explanation, his tousled yellow hair falling over his glasses. But that's not what Meg wanted to hear. She wanted to think about universal curves that showed up in different places, needing only people to notice their beauty.

Meg wondered if other people on the train spent as much time thinking about the curve of the power lines as she did. Maybe other people only liked to look out the window while the train was speeding through a town. Those people might think there was nothing to see outside the window once the train left the midwest, but they were wrong. Even as the train sped through miles of open fields and plains, the electrical wires were always there to watch. If the land seemed empty, that was the exciting thing about it. What a glory to belong to a country so huge there were vast stretches of land completely untamed except for the train tracks and swooping power lines. This was glorious American emptiness.

Japan wasn't like that. There was hardly any place in Japan that wasn't groomed for human use. Even the wild areas were manicured so they could be appreciated by priests and pilgrims.

Meg thought she could watch the swooping power line outside the window of the train forever without becoming bored. And she wasn't hypnotized either, just soothed, just comforted by the regularity of the lines which looked so much like they were moving when actually the lines were totally still. It was only the train that was moving.

Meg tried to list other things like that, which weren't moving but appeared to be because of the speed of something running along it. Or things that appeared to be still that were actually moving.

Probably the planet's rotation was something like that. When you lived on Earth, you couldn't feel it spinning. But if you were some kind of very slow space mole, digging out in the dark between the Earth and Mars, perhaps traveling clockwise around the Sun, the Earth would appear to spin and twirl.

Meg was infinitely more interested in what was happening outside the train window than inside the train car. Inside was pretty much just crackers and peanut butter and paper cups of water from the built-in dispenser.

Meg liked nighttime on the train best, when their seats were unfolded into bunks and curtains separated the bunks from the aisle. Throughout the night there was nothing to do other than to watch the swoop of the electrical lines illuminated by the moon. The swoop seemed to propel the train along like repetitive sling shots. "Move along, move along, move along," the swoops seemed to say.

There were places you could stand in America where no one had ever stood before. Meg wondered about each outcropping of rock or lump of a hill. Had anyone ever stood there before? Maybe a buffalo? Meg imagined she was seeing the sweep of time as she looked out the train window. There had been a time when only Indian tribes lived here, and hunted the buffalo, and brought skins back for their blankets and meat for their food.

Meg thought Father might like to look out at all this space after being captured and confined in Japan.

But Father preferred to talk with the people on the train. Meg supposed that was the freedom he was really hungry for, freedom from isolation. Even before the porters pulled the curtains open in the morning and tucked them neatly along the edges of the windows,

Father was up and off to the dining car for coffee and conversation.

Father particularly favored talking with the soldiers who were traveling from base to base. Father would ask the soldiers if they wanted to pray with him and receive his blessing. Invariably, they would say yes. Whatever their faith background, a blessing or prayer could be stored and stacked against whatever was to come.

Walter liked it when Father talked with soldiers, for a completely different reason. Walter had noticed that soldiers were the most likely passengers to have purchased a comic book wherever they boarded, and most likely to abandon it when they got off the train. Walter positioned himself close by when the soldiers pulled their duffels down from the overhead bins. More often than not, he heard "Here you go, kid" and a new comic book would be his. Sometimes the comics had mocking caricatures of Asian soldiers on the cover, but Walter would read them anyway, folding the front cover back so Father couldn't see.

There was one stop when Walter slid in to a seat to claim a magazine just a bit too soon. It turned out that the passenger had only gotten off the train to stretch his legs during a station stop and then he had hopped back on.

"Young man?" the man inquired of Walter.

"I'm sorry," Walter confessed. "I thought you were leaving this behind."

The magazine wasn't a comic. It was a popular science magazine.

"Interested in rockets, are you?" the man asked.

"Not really. Mostly cars and engines." Walter handed the man back his magazine and started to slide out into the aisle.

"No, no, have a seat. What's your name?"

The train pulled forward again. Walter and the man were soon deep in conversation about propulsion and fuel systems.

Gradually the scenery outside the window changed again. From seemingly endless plains, the land now seemed both more faded and sharper in its colors at the same time. Now the wild plants were a pale sage green, and the land was mostly tan and sand, although sometimes there were uprisings of rock striped with red and orange. Agile groups of petite elk dashed alongside the train and then fell away. Bumpy hills had been sliced in half for the train to go through. Off in the distance, Meg could see an exposed cliff with crumbled layers of different colors of soil. A clustered row of dusty green trees at the base suggested a river or streambed. Every once in a while, Meg caught a glimpse of a ranch house at the end of a dirt road.

The sky was huge, the vista limited only by the curve of the horizon. Meg could see at least three different types of clouds from her train window: streaked parallel rows, wispy drifting clouds, and enormous puffballs high up in the sky.

Walter was still in animated conversation with his new friend.

"If the Germans can build them, we can build better ones," Walter asserted.

The man agreed. "We can make anything we put our minds to."

The towns in New Mexico were like nothing Meg had seen. Square clay buildings with logs holding up the roofs. Some of the houses had outdoor ovens like giant clay beehives.

As they approached the station at Lamy, New Mexico, Meg could see a tiny fixed wing aircraft puttering through the sky. It drifted along next to the train for a moment, then climbed up and over the train, lost to Meg's sight. So that's how you would get home if you lived on one of those remote ranches, Meg thought with delight.

"Well, so long, Walter Binnenkerk." Walter's new friend stood to reach for his case up on the luggage rack as the train pulled in to the station.

"Thank you, Mr. Oppenheimer. Don't forget your magazine." Walter handed it up to him.

"Keep it, and read it."

"Thanks!"

Walter got what he wanted after all.


## *The Rocks*


Dr. Robert Oppenheimer stepped off the train at Lamy Station. He was headed to Santa Fe, and from there to a remote camp up on the Pajarito mesa. The area had once been the home of Keres-speaking Indians; now Los Alamos housed only a summer camp with a lodge and a few outbuildings. Dr. Oppenheimer had spent happy summer days riding horses in this back country. There was no better place he could think of to hide a secret nuclear weapons laboratory.

As soon as General Groves approved the location, it would be Dr. Oppenheimer's job to recruit the experts from around the country, whoever could translate the phenomenon of nuclear fission into a device for modern warfare. Dr. Oppenheimer tallied up in his mind who might be available to make the move to Los Alamos. Of course, they would have to agree to come without knowing why. Only when they arrived at the camp would they be told their mission: to produce a bomb that could be transported safely, triggered on demand, and fueled by a fast fission chain reaction. Dr. Oppenheimer was the "Coordinator of Rapid Rupture."

The U.S. had been smart to welcome scientists like Dr. Szilárd into the country. As far as Dr. Oppenheimer was concerned, émigré scientists were just as welcome as natural-born Americans to help on this project. Dr. Oppenheimer had worked in universities in America and Europe long enough to know that many of the best-trained most brilliant people were those who had been discarded by the Nazis. Dr. Oppenheimer looked around him at the mesa, envisioning how this isolated landscape was about to be transformed.

# Chapter 7
# A Home for Now

*Meg*

The scenery transformed again as the train sped west into Arizona. Now there were no trees in sight, except for the occasional windbreak planted by a farmer, but the colors of the dirt and rock were even more varied. They passed by dusky red rock formations. A couple of times Meg thought she saw Indians on spotted ponies riding on trails near the railroad tracks, but Meg thought she might have been dreaming that. The movement of the train was lulling her into an American dream.

Father broke Meg's reverie and told her to listen to the announcement.

"Next stop, Barstow, California."

Mother stood up to reach for her bag. Amy chose that moment to begin to cry. She could tell some kind of change was coming.

They lined up in the aisle, Father checking to make sure each of them had their bags. When the train came to a full stop, they stepped carefully onto the platform, feeling the strangeness of being still.

Barstow was tiny, just a main street and a few rows of houses. It was surprisingly hot for late autumn.

They were greeted by two pastors, both of whom wore short sleeve shirts, one in pink and one in light blue, buttoned up to the top with their clerical collars around the neck. Meg hadn't seen pastors wearing such light colors before. Both of them had sweat stains under their arms.

The pastors shook hands with Father and handed him a road map, a gas rations book, and the keys to a black car they pointed out in the dirt parking lot.

Meg thought she heard one of them say: "Watch out for the suicide doors."

While Father studied the road map, porters brought their two larger suitcases from the luggage compartment. Amy continued to wail as the pile of bags grew larger. Mother counted to make sure all of their bags had been unloaded.

The two pastors waved at Walter and Meg and hopped onto the train. They would get back to Los Angeles on the Santa Fe Chief.

"Why is it so hot?" Walter asked.

"Barstow's in the Mohave Desert," Father explained. "It will likely be cooler as we drive up into the mountains."

Their car was a black Plymouth sedan with a sloped back and a large trunk. Inside were two bench seats, one in the front and one in the back, and two sets of doors on each side, with their handles right next to each other. The doors opened like a cupboard.

Walter set up Amy's bassinet in the middle of the back seat. That way he and Meg would each get to sit by a window.

It didn't take long for the Binnenkerks to figure out what the pastors meant by "suicide doors." While

Father was pulling out of the parking lot, Walter opened his side door to free his shoelace. The wind caught the door and yanked it open, nearly pulling Walter out of the car and onto the pavement. Father slowed in a hurry, and Walter was able to close and latch the door.

In just a moment, Barstow was behind them. They passed through towns so small they just had a single gas station, motel, and restaurant. In between were fields of crops. Meg noticed a lake off to the right, but it was almost completely dry, surrounded by white patches that looked like salt. As they headed further north, a mountain range emerged in the distance on the left and another shorter range of mountains on the right. They were entering a broad valley between the two sets of mountains, but the mountains didn't match each other. The mountains on the left were jagged and craggy, with white drifts of snow capping their peaks and sliding down into the shady sides of rocky crevices. The mountains on the right were rounded and brown, dotted with sage green bushes. The road wound its way in between like a thin stream in a trough.

They passed through the town of Lone Pine. What a sad and romantic name, Meg thought to herself.

Luckily, there was more than one pine tree in the town, and she even saw some grassy meadows.

"We should be coming up to the camp now," Father said, jutting his chin to the left.

The first sign of Manzanar camp was a fence of barbed wire, incongruous because nothing else for miles around had been fenced. Then Meg could see a wooden tower with a platform and hut on top. It was a guard tower and sure enough, there were guards up high in the hut. Their long guns shimmered in the heat.

Meg craned her neck to look up at the sky around Manzanar. There weren't any planes in the sky. These guards weren't there to watch for the enemy coming down on them from the sky. They were watching the enemy living within the fence. They weren't there to protect the people living in Manzanar, but to trap them.

Through the fence, Meg could see rows and rows of wooden shacks. Had they not been aligned so precisely, had they instead been placed casually around the edge of a lake, they might have looked like summer cabins. But here they were lined up in ruler-straight rows with nothing but dust and rock in between.

"What a strange place to put people," Mother murmured.

Father didn't pull over to stop at the camp. The barbed wire fence flowed along parallel to the road and then abruptly turned left toward the snow-covered mountains. Suddenly Manzanar was out of sight. The landscape continued, brown and empty except for an orchard of dead trees.

The Binnenkerks were silent. To be fair, Amy was asleep, but the rest of them simply found they had nothing to say. The camp was a shock, like finding a dying animal by the side of a road.

Father sped up as they passed the orchard of dead trees. Why had the trees died, Meg wondered? Why was the lake they passed so dry? The mountains on the left were capped with snow. As hot as it was, there must have been ice melt flowing down the sides of the mountains, Meg thought. Why weren't the trees drinking it? Why didn't the lake fill up? It didn't make sense.

After a few miles, they saw a sign for the town of Independence. By now, their car was spitting out steam from around the hood. Father looked for a service station. When he pulled over next to the gas pump, a tall Negro gentleman came out from the station.

"Looks like you need more than gasoline," he said.

Father nodded. "Yes, we're lucky we made it here."

"May we please have some water for the radiator?" Walter asked from the back seat, showing off his knowledge of engines.

"Sure, sure. You'll just have to wait a while for the engine to cool down. The radiator will crack if you put in cold water while the engine's hot."

They all got out of the car to stretch. Father introduced himself to the gentleman, whose name was Mr. Evans.

"Is this your service station, Mr. Evans?" Father asked.

"Yessir. My family's lived in the Owens Valley for three generations. My grandfather was a cattleman."

"Now you take care of cars instead of horses," Walter said.

"That's about right. More horsepower," Mr. Evans said with a smile. "But there's not as much gasoline to sell any more, with the war on our doorstep."

Mr. Evans lifted the hood of their car. Pulling a bandana from the pocket of his overalls, Mr. Evans touched the radiator cap to see if had cooled down enough to take off.

"It'll be a while yet. Hey there," Mr. Evans gestured to Walter, "why don't you fill up that bucket with some water? The spigot's around the side."

Walter could see a blue bucket by the office door. He picked it up and went to find the spigot.

"You would have done a number on this engine if you had gone any further," Mr. Evans said to Father, shaking his head. "You have to carry extra water with you when you're driving long distances around here."

"I'll keep that in mind," Father said. "There shouldn't be too many long distances from now on."

"Is that right?"

"We're moving here to Independence."

"You don't say. Where're you living?"

Father told Mr. Evans the address of the house the Mission Board had rented for him.

"Well, that's just right around the block. You could walk there from here."

"Why don't we do that?" Father looked over at Mother. "Why don't we go look at the house and come back when the engine cools down?"

"That would be fine with me," Mr. Evans said. "I'm not likely to have another customer between now and then, and if I do, they could just pull up on the other side of the pump."

Walter set the bucket of water down on the ground next to the car. Mother lifted Amy out of the bassinet; she didn't awaken and just slumped in Mother's arms. Walter reached into the car to lift out the bassinet so they would have it at the house. Meg picked up the diaper bag and Mother's purse. The rest of their belongings could stay with the car.

It was a little cooler in Independence than it had been in Barstow, but not by much.

Independence was only a few blocks deep on the east side of the main street. The house was as easy to find as Mr. Evans promised. It was more a cabin than a house, Meg thought, but it had a sloped roof and was painted a friendly pale yellow. They mounted the two steps to a tiny front porch. The front door was locked, but Walter found the key on top of the black mailbox mounted on the wall.

Inside, the front room stretched across the width of the house. It was already furnished with a couch and upholstered chair on one side, and dining table and chairs on the other. A small square kitchen, one bathroom, and two bedrooms, one with a double bed, the other barely big enough for a single bed and a desk, made up the entirety of the house. Out the back door was a screened-in porch. That would suffice as Walter's bedroom on all but the coldest nights. Along the hallway were cupboards and drawers set into the wall for linens.

The house was stuffy and stale. Walter set down the bassinet, then he and Father went through every room and shoved open the windows. That accomplished, they headed back to the service station to see about the car.

Mother put Amy down in the bassinet.

"Well, it's by far the most cramped place we've ever lived," she remarked.

Meg chose to be hopeful. "That just means there'll be less to clean."

"Except for all this infernal dirt." Mother swept a finger along a windowsill and came away with gritty dust on her finger.

Meg started hunting for cleaning supplies. She came up with a broom and dust pan, mop and bucket.

"I'm sure those have seen plenty of use," Mother remarked.

Meg heard something in Mother's voice that reminded her of the sadness Mother had fallen into after

Amy was born, while Father was away. Mother had tried so hard to cheer up when Father was released. Meg was determined to keep that sadness at bay.

"You know what this reminds me of, Mother?"

"What's that?"

"The cabins at Lake Nojiri." Except that Independence was flat and the only lake was bleached dry.

"Well, now, that's a thought."

"And those were probably the happiest days of our family." Meg looked steadily at Mother. "We could be happy here too."

"Yes, we could," Mother reflected faintly, without looking at Meg. "I suppose we could."

Could happiness be chosen? Meg wondered. Could happiness at least be attempted?

There was barely time to fill the mop bucket in the kitchen and find some rags before Meg and Mother heard the car pull up the street and stop in front of the house. They went back outside to greet Father and Walter. The radiator was no longer steaming, but the black car had turned gray with the same dirt that coated everything in Independence.

Mother declared that nothing would be moved in until the house was clean, so the four of them spent the next hour wiping every surface and mopping every floor. Amy awoke with a start and watched wide-eyed.

Father mopped the kitchen floor first, so they could settle Amy on the floor with some toys while Mother and Meg wiped down the kitchen shelves and drawers.

Soon Father was coughing so badly from the dust and grit in the air that Mother sent him away to find the grocer while she and Meg put the linens on the beds.

Left alone in the kitchen, Amy began to cry. She crawled into the hallway and pulled herself up to standing, holding onto the draw pulls of the linen drawers set into the hallway. And there she stood, sobbing, until Mother and Meg finished making up the bigger bed; Meg lay Amy on it to change her soggy diaper and wipe her tear-stained face.

"Look what I found!" Walter called from the backyard. There was a shed in the back, and inside it, a bicycle. The seat was torn and the chain caked with black grease. All the metal parts were rusty and the tires were flat. Walter dug around for an empty can to soak the chain.

"I'll just need some oil, steel wool, and pliers to straighten out the pedals." He dove back into the shed to see if he could find what he needed. If he could get the bike in working condition, Walter thought, he could have some independence in Independence.

## *The Rocks*

Not all uranium atoms split. Most uranium atoms could absorb a neutron without splitting. Swallowing a neutron made the uranium atom really lopsided and unstable, though. Over time, it would fidget and shed a couple of neutrons without splitting in two. Scientists called this process radioactive decay.

It was a Canadian-American scientist named Dr. Arthur Jeffrey Dempster who helped explain why some uranium atoms split and others didn't. He developed a magnetic mass analyzer that could count the exact number of particles like neutrons and protons in an atom of uranium. It turned out that not all uranium was the same. Most uranium had 92 protons and 146 neutrons in each nucleus, giving it a total mass of 238.

That kind of uranium could absorb a neutron without splitting.

A much rarer isotope of uranium had 3 fewer neutrons. U235 was the fissile stuff, the variety of uranium that could split. Most uranium ore found in nature, including the Shinkolobwe rocks, were made up mostly of U238 and just a little U235.

Now the scientists knew it was the U235 in Dr. Hahn's experiments that had burst. But that didn't mean the more plentiful U238 was useless. American chemist Dr. Glenn T. Seaborg watched U238 closely through its journey of radioactive decay. As it adjusted and shed neutrons, U238 settled into a new element altogether. Dr. Seaborg named this new element plutonium, and it was fissile, too. Washing away the U238 through painstaking chemical processes in his laboratory, Dr. Seaborg was able to isolate the tiniest speck of plutonium.

U235 burst and released a couple of neutrons, so theoretically, it could support a nuclear chain reaction. But when plutonium burst, each nucleus almost always released 3 neutrons. Even if some of those neutrons spun away, there were enough to sustain a super-fast chain reaction. In other words, plutonium was even more fissile than U235.

# Chapter 8
# It's Worth a Try

*Meg*

Eventually, Father said yes. It was an early Sunday morning when Father said Meg could go into the Manzanar relocation camp with him.

Father was preoccupied, as he usually was when he had his clergy collar on, so Meg said nothing on the drive from Independence to the camp.

Father parked outside the fence. Meg followed him up to the pedestrian gate. Father spoke to the guard and the gate was opened for them, and then shut behind them. Now Meg and Father were locked in the camp.

First, Father took Meg to the camp office, a squat stone building just inside the gate. At the front desk was a tiny woman. Father introduced her as Miss Moroni.

She was dwarfed by her giant desk, surrounded by stacks of paper, but she had a tight, courteous smile for Meg and Father. Miss Moroni had long hair wrapped in a bun on the top of her head, probably hoping her hair would add a few inches to her height.

Meg wondered why Miss Moroni was working at the office on a Sunday. Maybe weekends didn't mean anything when you were running a camp. After all, the prisoners were there all day, every day.

Miss Moroni stepped out from behind her giant desk and picked up a stack of church bulletins. Meg realized she was going to walk to the camp church with them.

Father and Meg stepped out of the stone building and headed into the camp. All the dirt pathways in the camp looked the same to Meg, some heading west toward the mountains and some heading north and south parallel to the highway. Father pointed out the numbers on the wooden sheds; that was how Meg could keep from getting lost. The Protestant church was in Block 15.

Now Meg could see camp residents everywhere. Some were sitting on the stoops of the barracks. Others were standing in line for the washrooms or a water spigot. Others were scrubbing clothes in tubs and hanging them on clotheslines. Every face was Japanese.

Unaccountably, Meg was drenched in a wave of joy. Meg knew she should have felt sad or scared for the Japanese-Americans being held against their will. But Meg hadn't seen a single Japanese face for more than a year. For Meg, the unfamiliar had suddenly turned familiar.

So this is where Meg's people were. Meg felt her eyes prick with tears. She didn't know any of these people, but they were more family to her than any of the guards.

Block 15 was just another shack, just the same as the ones next to it. Its walls were bare wooden boards, some slightly curved, leaving cracks and crevices. Inside were no pews, just metal folding chairs. Most of the church leaders were Japanese-Americans living in the camp, but there was one other visiting Protestant missionary, Pastor Wormley. He shook Meg's hand enthusiastically.

"Do you have your family here too?" Meg asked him.

"No, I'm only assigned here for a year, so I left my family behind."

Pastor Wormley was younger than Father, and had a bit of a belly, unusual for a younger man. He was also starting to get a bald spot on the top of his head.

"Are you living in Independence or Lone Pine?" Meg asked.

"Neither. Since I'm here by myself, I'm in a staff bunkhouse inside the camp."

"You don't have a car, then," Meg guessed.

"That's right. All my meals are taken care of, and if I need to go somewhere, I can always ask for a ride." Pastor Wormley turned to greet the parishioners as they arrived for the service. Meg slipped away to help set up chairs.

Meg saw Miss Moroni with the church bulletins standing next to Pastor Wormley. He shook hands and bowed to the parishioners and she handed each family a bulletin.

Once the worship service began, it was like church anywhere. Meg could close her eyes and be in church in Tsu or Lake Nojiri or Michigan. The same hymns. The same liturgy. Where two or three were gathered, Jesus had said, that's where the church was. The church was here.

Meg's heart lifted to see Father back at the lectern. He spoke and sang in both English and Japanese, welcoming the Holy Spirit. This church had more people than Meg remembered seeing in the tiny mission church in Japan, but perhaps that wasn't surprising. The people living in the camp were Americans, after all. More of them were Christians.

Meg noticed a girl sitting in the middle of the congregation. Actually, it wasn't so much that Meg noticed her but that Meg noticed the girl deliberately refusing to notice Meg. The girl would slide her gaze sideways toward Meg and then deliberately turn her head forward.

What had she done to offend her? Meg had just arrived in the camp and hadn't spoken to anyone except the secretary and Pastor Wormley.

When the service was over, Meg decided to take the initiative.

Meg walked up to the girl's side and said hello in Japanese. "Konnichiwa."

The girl looked flatly over at Meg. "I speak better English than you do."

"OK, then, well, hello." Meg figured her English was pretty close to perfect but saw no point in contradicting the girl.

"How are you doing today?" Meg made another attempt.

"Why do you care?" The girl had turned to face Meg now. Actually, it was more confronting than facing.

"Well, there aren't many people our age here. I mean, there are a lot of older people, and littler kids." Meg was running out of courage. "I thought we could get to know each other."

"You want to be friends with me." The girl's expression was blank.

Meg's heart sank. She hadn't succeeded at making any friends in Zeeland. Was it going to be that hard here too?

"Yes," said Meg. "I mean, why not?"

"You think we can be friends."

"Yes. Why wouldn't we?"

The girl seemed almost ready to refuse. Then she stuck out her right hand to shake Meg's. "Deanna Matsumoto."

"Hello. I'm Meg Binnenkerk."

"Hi." Deanna just looked at Meg, waiting for Meg to take the next step.

"What is there to do around here after church?" Meg ventured.

"Not much."

"My father is the new chaplain here." Meg gestured with her chin toward the altar. "How about your family?"

"Before the war we had a seafood store. Now, my Dad's trying to make furniture out of whatever wood he can find."

"Where do you get the wood?"

"There's a scrap pile behind the dining hall, although why they call it a dining hall is beyond me."

"What do you mean?"

"It isn't exactly fine dining."

"I guess they could call it a chow hall."

"We call it a mess hall, because the food's a mess."

Meg laughed at that. "Let's go find the pile of wood and see if we can find any good boards for your Dad," Meg suggested. Meg found Father and asked permission. Father looked over at Deanna's father, who gave a very slight nod.

"Be back here in an hour," Father said. "Don't go too close to the guard towers."

Meg knew that Father actually meant things like "Don't make me ashamed of your behavior" and "Don't undermine the relationships we're building here." Meg knew the rules of being a minister's kid.

"I won't go near the guard towers," Meg promised.

The girls slipped past the parishioners and out of the church barracks. Meg followed as Deanna threaded her way through the dusty lanes to the mess hall. Behind it was a pile of discarded boards. A few were full length pieces of timber, left over from building the barracks. Most were broken lengths of wood. There were also piles of used vegetable crates with narrower wooden slats.

There was another person hunting around to see what scraps could be used.

Deanna nodded toward him. "That's Mr. Fujii. He is a gardener here."

Meg bowed and the elderly gentleman bowed back. Deanna switched to Japanese to ask the old man what he was looking for. He answered and Deanna turned to Meg to translate what he said.

"I understood him, Deanna," Meg interrupted. "He's looking for some stakes to make cages for the chrysanthemums in his greenhouse." It actually was harder for Meg to understand Mr. Fujii than she let on. Meg was shocked to realize how much Japanese she had forgotten. It had been more than a year since she left Japan. Meg had been so determined to stop using Japanese to fit in better in Michigan. She was paying a price for that now, Meg thought ruefully.

"Well, good for you," Deanna retorted.

Meg ignored Deanna's tone of voice. "Probably he would want bamboo, but I'm sure we won't find any of that here. Let's help him."

The girls started climbing through the pile. Fujii-san pointed at strips of wood he wanted to look at, and Meg and Deanna pulled them out of the stacks so the elderly man didn't have to rummage through the unstable pile.

There were boys sitting on the back stoop of the mess hall watching them clamber over the wood pile. "Looking good, doll," one of the boys called to Deanna.

"Take a powder, Romeo," Deanna called back.

"Is his name really Romeo?" Meg whispered to Deanna.

"No, his name is Yasuo. He just has delusions of grandeur."

The other boys smirked at Yasuo and he punched one of them on the arm. Then Yasuo stood up and slunk off the porch.

"See you later, Yasuo," the boys called after him.

"Mata ne," he muttered.

Mr. Fujii ignored the boys, focusing on the pile of wood slats the girls were stacking. He nodded and bowed, satisfied, and carried away a surprisingly large stack for such a tiny old man.

On the way back toward Block 15, Meg and Deanna passed a tiny garden made out of rocks balanced and stacked to look like a little pagoda temple. A pipe spilled water into a large basin lined with cement, which spilled over into another. Around the edges, plants had been carefully placed in the ground and tended. None of them were blooming now. The growing season was long over, but some of the stems and vines were still green.

"This is amazing," Meg blurted out. "What a sweet little garden!"

"Cute, huh?"

Meg looked at Deanna and said so in Japanese: "Kawaii!"

"Hai,-sōdesune," Deanna agreed.

Meg smiled. It was fun to talk with someone who could switch back and forth between English and Japanese.

"Who else from your family is here in Manzanar?" Meg asked.

"Both my parents, my grandparents, and my brother Frank. He wasn't living with us in California. He was already away at college. But now we're all stuck here together."

"That's crummy that he had to drop out of school."

"Yup, he's pretty steamed about it."

"But nice that you all get to be together," Meg said, trying to find something positive to say.

"Yeah, living in a shack in the middle of nowhere."

"Actually, the middle of nowhere is over in Independence. This is more like the far edge of nowhere."

Deanna looked at Meg as though she wasn't sure Meg was joking. Then she cracked a smile. "That sounds like a radio show. I would actually listen to that – The Far Edge of Nowhere ...."

"Was your brother at church this morning?" Meg hadn't remembered seeing any young man with Deanna.

"He told Mom and Dad he wasn't going. Mostly he hangs out, doing nothing."

"What do your parents think about that?"

"There's a lot of arguing about him wasting his life. But then again, we're all wasting our lives here."

Wanting to change the subject, Meg decided to take another chance.

"Why were you ignoring me back at church?"

Deanna looked up at Meg with an expression on her face. It was something like sarcasm and something like guilt.

"You get that you're the only white girl here, don't you?"

"Yeah. So?"

"Well, I had a white friend in L.A. where I grew up. I mean, I had a lot of friends and practically all of them were white, but I had a best friend! Shirley!"

Deanna was getting herself all worked up. She took a deep breath.

Meg asked, "So what happened?"

"You know what happened!" Deanna exploded. "All that talk about Japs and yellow traitors!" Deanna looked around, suddenly realizing that others might have heard her. "As if we weren't already planning to try out for majorettes this year! As if we hadn't been hanging out at recess practicing baton twirling together for years!"

"She just stopped talking to you?"

"She stopped acting like I existed. If I was walking down the hall, she would stop and talk to someone else and turn her back toward me. If we were both waiting for the school bus, the bus we had sat together on for years, she would get out of line, actually get out of line, and go sit on a bench until I got on the bus. Then she would get on last and sit as far away from me as she possibly could."

"What about when the deportation order went up?"

"Nothing. She never said good-bye. I still had a pair of her shoes at my house from the last time she slept over. They had gotten all wet at the beach and she ended up going home in her socks."

"Well, there's that," Meg reasoned. "Now she'll never get her shoes back."

Deanna almost cracked a smile. "Yeah, that'll teach her – she won't get her shoes back."

"Poor Shirley," Meg said, smiling.

"Yeah, poor Shoeless Shirley." Now they were both laughing.

"I guess you thought I would be like Shirley?" Meg ventured.

"I guess so."

"Well, you should have known better. Look," Meg said, pointing toward her feet. "I've got shoes."

"Yeah, no Shoeless Shirleys here. Hey, world!" Deanna yelled. "We've got shoes! We may not have much of anything else but we have shoes!"

"Have shoes - will conquer the world!" Meg yelled.

"We're shoeful! We got shoes - how's about yous?" Deanna yelled at the sky.

"Meg?" Deanna asked when they regained their breath.

"Yeah?"

"What are you doing here anyway? You're not Japanese."

"I told you. My father's the chaplain."

"I know, but how come you aren't making friends over in Independence? How come they even let you into this palace?" Deanna asked, sweeping her hand grandly to take in the rows of wooden shacks and dusty pathways.

"They let me in because I came with my father."

"But they'll also let you out. You get to go home."

"Yeah, I get to go home."

"So, why did you come here if you don't have to?"

Meg shrugged. "Curious."

"What grade are you in?"

"I'm still in junior high. You?"

'High school. Well, I started high school before the order went up."

They had reached the front of the camp, where the teenaged boys were playing basketball with an improvised hoop. To Meg's eye, it was the rim of a barrel nailed to a board.

"There's my brother." Deanna pointed. "Hey, Frank!"

Frank nodded back and passed the ball to a teammate, who fumbled and dropped it.

"Go away, Deanna," Frank called. "You're distracting my team."

"Well, that's your problem, isn't it?" Deanna tossed her long black hair over her shoulder. "C'mon, Meg, let's go."

When they reached Block 15, Meg started climbing the steps to go back to Father, but Deanna had one more thing to say.

"Hey, Meg, why did the chicken cross the road?"

"Why?"

"To get out of Manzanar!"

"That's a good one, Deanna."

Deanna sauntered off. Meg entered the church and found her father. He was deep in conversation with Pastor Wormley. That was no surprise, to find Father in conversation. Meg settled down to wait.

The was a feeling swirling up inside Meg. A feeling of surprise. It was a miracle, actually. Meg had wanted to make a friend since she left Japan. Frankly, she had wanted a friend long before that. She and Walter had mostly been on their own at the mission house in Tsu, and Meg only saw her mission cousins during the summers at Lake Nojiri.

Now she had made a friend, and it hadn't been that hard to do. All Meg had to do was go over and say hello, and put up with a little rudeness.

There was something special about Deanna, that was for sure. Deanna was blunt. She talked with boys carelessly, as if she didn't care whether they liked her or not. Deanna had a community she belonged to, even if her whole neighborhood had been relocated to this strange place.

Meg tried to put a label on what she was feeling. It was relief. Maybe Deanna couldn't wait to leave Manzanar, but Meg couldn't wait to come back.

## *The Rocks*

Dr. Enrico Fermi was building a different kind of pile. His wasn't made of wood, like the pile behind the Manzanar camp mess hall. Dr. Fermi's pile was made of the three ingredients for a nuclear chain reaction.

Dr. Fermi had been Italy's finest physicist. When the Italian fascists joined the Nazis, Dr. Fermi tried to leave Rome with his wife and children, but the Italian government wouldn't let them go. Fortuitously, Dr. Fermi won the Nobel Prize in 1938, and that meant he and his family were invited to Sweden to accept the award. The Italian government was all too glad to approve that trip for one of their most famous citizens. The Fermis packed light and never returned. They came to America where they were welcomed.

Now, working closely with Dr. Szilárd, Dr. Fermi had managed to gather the ingredients for a chain reaction. They had a radium concoction to release a stream of neutrons. They had a buffer, not of wax but of very pure bricks of graphite, to slow the flow of neutrons down and keep the neutrons close to the fissile material. And they had metallic plugs and cans of uranium. Dr. Fermi had practiced stacking the graphite blocks and uranium in a variety of configurations. For this test, he had settled on a giant beehive-shaped pile using 45,000 graphite blocks.

Of course, there was a fourth ingredient any nuclear reaction had to have: a way to slow and stop a chain reaction. The last thing Dr. Fermi wanted was a runaway explosion of radiation. Some safety precautions were in order.

With safety in mind, Dr. Fermi and Dr. Szilárd moved their experiments from Columbia University in New York City to an enclosed, windowless squash court deep in the concrete football stadium at the University of Chicago. Second, they assembled their pile of graphite bricks and uranium slugs inside a thick rubber tent the shape of a giant cube. This tent was twenty-five square feet, with a front curtain that could be rolled all the way up or down.

What Dr. Fermi really needed, though, wasn't just a way to contain a chain reaction, but to interrupt and stop it. He turned to cadmium, an element which is a known neutron hog. His team nailed thin strips of cadmium metal to wooden slats that they could slide in and out of the pile in the gaps between the stacked bricks. The idea was that when the cadmium rods were pushed all the way into the pile, they would absorb all the loose neutrons being emitted by the radium concoction, starving the uranium and stopping any chain reaction.

The uranium Dr. Fermi and Dr. Szilárd were using was the natural mix of U238 and U235. No one had figured out yet how to separate U235 from U238. Even so, Dr. Fermi was worried enough about the volatile U235 in the mix to add a few more safety precautions. The scientists hung a cadmium rod above the pile, connected to a rope on a pulley. Cutting the rope would drop the rod into the center of the stack. And they kept a bucket of liquid cadmium handy to fling over the pile.

Most of the members of Dr. Fermi's team watched from up on the squash court balcony. One unlucky candidate had to stay below with the bucket of liquid cadmium and the ax to cut the rope. That person was most at risk. Everyone knew an explosion of runaway radiation would definitely not be good for human beings.

Using graphite as a moderator instead of wax made sense to the scientists, but this wasn't the same graphite you see in the core an ordinary pencil. This graphite had to be ground up and any impurities sifted out, then shaped into building bricks carved with semi-circular pockets for the uranium plugs. This was definitely a product the National Carbon Company had never made before, and now they had an order for four hundred tons of it.

The Goodyear Rubber Company had never made a cube-shaped rubber tent three stories high before either. Obviously, Dr. Fermi and Dr. Szilárd couldn't just go shopping for items like these in any store, but General Groves could get it for them. Everything changed for the scientists once they had the backing of President Roosevelt and the U.S. government. American companies were proud to help.

The pile wasn't going to jiggle or vibrate if a chain reaction started. It was going to emit energy in the form of radiation. That wouldn't be visible, so measuring it fell to an American physicist named Dr. Leona Woods. She planted radiation sensors throughout the pile and kept the detectors with her on the balcony. Any release of radiation would send her counters ticking. That way, everyone could hear how slowly or quickly a chain reaction was happening.

December 2, 1942 was the day for the full-scale experiment. It had taken a few days for the college students helping out to stack all the bricks to Dr. Fermi's specifications. The cadmium rods were all in place pushed deep into the pile. When it was time to begin, Dr. Fermi instructed his assistants to slide out all but one of the cadmium rods. Nothing happened. Dr. Fermi gave the instruction to slide the last cadmium stick out slowly, six inches at a time.

Dr. Woods' radiation detectors twitched.

Fission fizzed, then fizzled out. Dr. Fermi gave the instruction for the last cadmium stick to come out another six inches. And stop. Then a little more. Then stop.

At that point, Dr. Fermi no longer believed it would be necessary to drop the rubber curtain or throw cadmium liquid over the pile. The cadmium sticks seemed adequate to control the pace of the neutron release and absorption. Fairly confident that the experiment would work, Mr. Fermi called a lunch break. There was no point in making history with a hungry crew. The scientists slid the cadmium sticks back into the pile and the crew headed up into the sunlight.

What they didn't know was that the Germans were experimenting with using graphite as a moderator, too. But the Germans didn't have tons of it, like Dr. Fermi and Dr. Szilárd, and theirs hadn't been adequately purified.

The Germans built a much smaller pile of graphic bricks and uranium, but contaminants in the graphite interfered with the flow and slow of neutrons. The neutrons skipped right off the uranium. No chain reaction. That's when the Germans made a crucial mistake. Instead of realizing all they needed to do was purify the graphite, the Germans gave up on using graphite altogether. They turned their attention to other possible moderators. Giving up on graphite was a critical error and slowed their scientific progress. The Americans didn't know it at the time, but the U.S. had taken the lead in the race to build a nuclear bomb.

After lunch, Dr. Fermi's crew walked back across the quad, entered the stadium, and descended down to the squash court. Dr. Fermi again directed the process of sliding the cadmium control sticks out of their tunnels of uranium-pocketed graphite. Without the cadmium to absorb the neutrons, the uranium began to catch some neutrons - absorb, fission, release, absorb, fission, release. Dr. Woods' counters ticked and buzzed, reporting a steady release of radiation. It was a sustained chain reaction, emitting hardly enough energy to light up a lightbulb, but it was working.

A slow and steady reaction like this one produces energy, and the experiment definitely generated more energy than it takes to make a grain of sand hop. Dr. Fermi and his crew had created the world's first nuclear reactor. They had harnessed the power of a subatomic transformation of mass to energy.

What they made was a pile, not a bomb. A pile uses slow fission; a bomb needs a fast fission reaction. But Dr. Fermi and his colleagues had proven that a nuclear chain reaction was not just a theory. It worked.

Dr. Woods looked over at Dr. Fermi and asked, "When do we become scared?"

# Chapter 9
# Chain Reaction

## *Meg*

A chain reaction of sorts was happening inside Manzanar, too. Because of it, Father wouldn't let Meg go back with him into the camp.

"There's been some trouble," Father said.

"What do you mean?" Meg demanded.

"There's a dispute brewing in the food area."

"You mean the food is making people sick?" That wouldn't have surprised Meg, given Deanna's comments about the mess hall.

"No, about whether food is being sold to people outside the camp rather than being fed to the residents."

"Someone is stealing the camp's food?"

"There are accusations. And those aren't the only problems in camp right now."

"What do you mean?"

Father side-stepped the question. "I'll take you back in when it's safer for you."

"But Deanna will be expecting me." They had just met, but Meg didn't want Deanna to think she was a fair-weather friend, like Shirley.

Father wouldn't hear any argument. "It's not a safe place for a little girl right now."

If it wasn't safe for Meg then it wasn't safe for Deanna, Meg thought.

Walter's bicycle was looking a bit more functional. He had scraped all the rust off the frame, but that ended up scraping off most of the paint, too, leaving the bike a dull silver. Walter pushed the bike over to Mr. Evans' service station and used his air pump to fill up the tires. They seemed to hold the air pretty well, so the bike was rideable, if not particularly pretty. On Sunday, after church in Independence, Meg thought she might explore the town with Walter, but he pedaled ahead and Meg couldn't keep up.

That afternoon, Mother and Amy were nestled in a large chair in the living room. Mother had begun to volunteer in the tiny Independence library, and she had checked out just about every baby book in the collection to read to Amy. Meg left the house and wandered around Independence by herself, wishing she could go back into Manzanar.

Over the next week, things got worse in the camp. There was a fight between a group of residents. One of the Japanese-Americans was badly hurt.

Meg hardly saw Father. He was spending all his time at the camp, trying to help calm the situation down, but Father was new and there wasn't a lot of trust to go around.

"Why would the residents beat up one of their own people?" Walter asked.

"The victim was one the leaders," Father said. "It's a tough spot for Japanese-Americans leaders to be in. They don't really have the power to negotiate with the American military, but they try, and then the other prisoners think they're in cahoots with the authorities."

The next evening when Father came home, his face was ashen. Crowds of prisoners had formed around the police station and hospital, making demands. Soldiers had assembled around them. As the crowd grew angrier, the soldiers fired tear gas and the Japanese-Americans began to scatter and run. In the chaos, some of the soldiers fired their guns. Several of the Japanese-Americans had been shot and one was dead.

"Who was shot?" Meg demanded. "Any of the Matsumotos?"

"No, no, Meg. They're fine." Father showered and prepared to go back in, this time to meet with the families of the injured and dead. Meg knew better than to even ask to go with him.

Meg waited. In the week that followed, another of the young men who had been shot died of his wounds. The Manzanar riot was reported in the news as an uprising by Japanese-Americans loyal to Tokyo.

"What did any of it have to do with Tokyo?" Meg wanted to know.

"Nothing," Father said.

"Why would the news say so then?"

Mother answered, "It's a way to make the Japanese-Americans look disloyal to America, to justify having locked them up." It was probably the least charitable thing Meg had ever heard Mother say. Meg looked over at Father, but he didn't contradict her.

A Buddhist funeral was held for the two dead men. Finally, on Christmas Eve, Father said they could go back to Manzanar as a family for the Christian service. Amy wore a soft wool coat with a matching hat that had little felt bear ears sewn on top. Mother wore her best hat and gloves.

They walked together down the bitter dusty path to the barracks. The church was filling rapidly with parishioners, as well as camp employees and even a few of the guards. Camp Director Merritt sat up front and Miss Moroni helped Pastor Wormley pass out the hymnals and bulletins.

Father read the Bible from the pulpit. "And it came to pass in those days, that there went out a decree from Caesar Augustus that all the world should be taxed. And Joseph went up from Galilee, out of the City of Nazareth, into Judea, unto the City of David, which is called Bethlehem, because he was of the house and lineage of David, to be taxed with Mary his espoused wife, being great with child."

Father cleared his throat, looked up, and spoke slowly. "They were ordered to move because the government said so, even though it was a burden to them, even though Mary was about to have her baby. And it was not an easy journey, as many of you may imagine."

Meg looked up at Father. He wasn't talking just about Mary and Joseph any more. Father was speaking to Japanese-Americans held in captivity because of their lineage, because of the decree of a government, no matter whether they were very old or babies.

"And when they got to Bethlehem, Mary and Joseph did not receive much of a welcome. There was no place for them in the inn. The only place they could find to give birth to the Son of God was a lowly stable."

Father looked up at his congregation. "I have spoken with many of you since arriving here at Manzanar. You know what it is like to have no lodging other than a stable. Many of you were held in the horse stalls on the race track in Los Angeles while Manzanar was being built. Your lodgings here are humble wooden dwellings, indeed."

"I pray that you will remember this Christmas holiday what Mary and Joseph learned so long ago, that the Son of God didn't need a place of luxury to be born. The greatest glory of their young lives came in a place more humble than this, as troubled as this, as frightening for their young family as this place is for yours."

"As Christians, we believe the world was saved because Mary and Joseph welcomed that child. And so, we all welcome each other to this place, as humble as it is, as separated as we are from everything we used to call home. Because what we know is this: God works miracles in places just like this."

The congregation sang "Silent Night" in English, and then in Japanese. "Kiyoshi kono yoru." Pure, holy night.

Father and Pastor Wormley offered communion that night. Meg slipped out of line to go up for communion with Deanna. Deanna squeezed her hand and Meg felt awash in relief. Deanna didn't blame her for staying away. They were still friends.

Tonight, Deanna had left her long black hair loose. When she knelt to receive the bread and grape juice, her hair drifted over her shoulders and draped down the sides of her face. She bowed her head gracefully, looking for all the world like a Japanese Mary. Meg felt clunky and awkward next to her, but still she was happy to be with Deanna again. Meg followed Deanna back to her seat and sat with her family until the end of the service. If all of them were very lucky, both the Americans and the Japanese-Americans, the chain reaction of fear and distrust in the camp could be stopped.

## *The Rocks*

Now the scientists knew the uranium that fissioned after neutron capture was U235. And they knew plutonium derived from U238 was even more fissile than that.

That meant there were two pathways to a bomb. One route involved trying to separate the U235 from the U238. Maybe they couldn't get to pure U235, but at least a higher proportion of U235 in the mix. The second route involved feeding neutrons to U238, allowing it to decay into plutonium, and painstakingly separating the plutonium from the spent U238. Then plutonium could become the core of a bomb.

Which path should the U.S. take? To General Groves, that was a trick question. The answer was both, of course.

Was it even possible to separate U235 from U238? The only difference between the two isotopes was three neutrons. There were a few ideas floating around about how to pull it off. Of course, if you asked General Groves which method the U.S. should try, his answer would be all of them, of course.

And what about manufacturing plutonium? Dr. Seaborg had isolated plutonium by bombarding U238 with neutrons in a particle accelerator and then teasing away the spent U238 to leave a barely visible crumb of plutonium. The other way was to trigger radioactive decay in U238 through a reactor pile, like the kind Dr. Fermi and Dr. Szilárd built in Chicago. The radiated uranium from the reactor pile would have to be cooled before it could be handled, but then harsh chemicals could be used to dissolve away the spent uranium and extract the plutonium a few micro-grams at a time.

Obviously, General Groves wanted to pursue both methods, and he didn't want any laboratory-sized particle accelerator or a reactor pile with a measly 45,000 bricks of graphite. He wanted particle accelerators the size of football fields. He wanted reactors the size of ocean liners. Because the goal wasn't to manufacture a few micro-grams of plutonium. General Groves wanted full grams of plutonium, pounds of plutonium, maybe even a ton of plutonium. General Groves wanted plutonium factories bigger than New York's Cunard building.

Here's where the U.S. pulled away from all its competitors vying to make a bomb. Yes, scientists in Germany were experimenting with prototype-sized piles. For sure, they had laboratory-sized particle accelerators, but building anything bigger than that would have definitely drawn attention and become a target for Allied aerial bombing raids. By contrast, the U.S. had 48 states and territories far from fighting, far from prying eyes, and wide flowing rivers which could generate enough electrical power to run these factories and cool off the hot nuclear reactions.

When U.S. industry muscled up for this fight, no other country could touch them. No one could match the scale of the resources the Americans were investing in this bomb. There was no question. The U.S. was going to have the best nuclear toys in the world.

# Chapter 10
# Toys

*Meg*

The Quakers had donated Christmas toys for the children of Manzanar. The toys arrived at the church in Independence after the holiday, but Meg and Walter were happy to help unload the truck. Among the toys were a dozen or so tricycles. Some were brand new, others were scratched and worn but had plenty of use left.

Walter looked them over and then told Meg, "I'll be right back."

He rode his bike over to the service station.

"Hi Mr. Evans."

"Hello there, Walter. How's that bike of yours?"

Walter looked down at his bike. "It's running well. That's kind of what I wanted to talk with you about."

"Oh?"

"There were some toys donated for the children in Manzanar, including some tricycles, and they need a coat of paint. I was wondering if I could work for you on Saturdays in trade for some paint."

"Well, Walter, I dunno."

"I don't have school on Saturdays. I could pump the gas, wash windows, run the air pump."

"I don't doubt you could do those things, Walter, but I can't have a kid running the pumps, and I don't know about the air either. People's tires are pretty thin these days. It takes a careful hand to fill the air without going too far."

"Washing windows then?" Walter pushed a little harder. "Wouldn't that be great if you could just focus on pumping the gas when a customer comes in, and their windshield is all clean by the time you're done?"

"Well, I suppose." Walter could tell that something was holding Mr. Evans back.

"Walter, I don't mind giving you some paint for your bicycle, but as for the other  bikes… that camp you're talking about. That's the one between here and Lone Pine?"

"Yes, sir."

"You hear what they say, Walter. How come the people in the camp get to have hand-outs during wartime when everyone else is doing without?"

At least he didn't call them Japs, Walter thought.

"I don't know if it's handouts, Mr. Evans, when we made them leave their homes and leave everything behind."

Walter was careful not to say, "They're Americans just like you and me." For all he knew, Mr. Evans had relatives in the war. Still, it was just toys for children, who hadn't done anything wrong.

"Sir, all I'm asking you for is a can of metal paint, and maybe some turpentine."

"I suppose no one has to know what it's for."

Oh, thought Walter, it wasn't so much that Mr. Evans was against helping, but that he was worried what his customers would think.

Walter had learned that sometimes just standing still was the most effective way to get what he wanted. Walter stood still.

"Well, alright, you got yourself a deal. I think I've got a can of paint around here somewhere that will work on metal. Let's go see."

This was more than Walter expected. "But I haven't earned it yet."

"You might as well take it now. I'll expect you Saturdays. Those are busy days for me and I could use the help." That last statement might have been pushing the truth. Mr. Evans' place was a sleepy little gas station in a tiny town at a time when most people had limited gas rations, but Walter wasn't going to push his luck.

"Thank you, sir." Walter followed Mr. Evans into the garage. Mr. Evans reached up on a dusty shelf in the storeroom and handed Walter an unopened can of bright red paint. "Don't have much use for this color anyway. Most folks like their cars black and their tractors green."

He handed Walter a half-full tin can of turpentine and a couple of brushes. "These brushes are meant for oil. They aren't really paint brushes, but they're clean and they'll do."

"Thank you, Mr. Evans." Now Walter was wondering how he could carry it all. Walter stuffed the brushes in his back pocket and tucked the can of turpentine under his arm. He could hold the paint can in that hand and still have a hand to steer the bike.

Walter pushed off to ride back to the church. "Thanks again, Mr. Evans. I'll see you on Saturday morning."

"Don't mention it," Mr. Evans called, and he probably meant exactly that.

Walter wobbled his way back to the church, wishing he had a basket for his bike. Then, leaving the bike and supplies on the stoop, he went inside to choose the tricycles most in need of a new coat of paint.

One of the deacons helped Walter roll the tricycles out to where there was a bit of sidewalk along the side of the church. Soon, Walter had a couple of the high school boys helping too, in assembly-line fashion, one of them cleaning each tricycle with soapy water, another checking and tightening bolts, another sanding any rust off those that needed to be painted, and finally Walter making the can of paint last as long as he could. There would soon be an impressive fleet of tricycles ready for delivery into Manzanar.

Father let both Walter and Meg help with the delivery. He had arranged for one of the camp trucks to pick up the load of toys in Independence and carry them into the camp. Director Merritt let them drive the truck right into the camp to make the unloading easier. Most of the toys went to the toy loan center. The rest, including the tricycles, went to the church barracks.

Meg and Walter climbed up into the back of the truck to hand the toys down. Deanna and Frank showed up to help, along with some of the other older boys.

"Here you go!" Meg tried to hand a bike down to Yasuo, but he was deaf to Meg. His eyes were locked on Deanna.

Deanna grabbed the bike from Meg and pushed it at Yasuo. "Rise and shine!"

After the toys were unloaded and the truck pulled away with a belch of diesel smoke, Meg and Deanna wandered over to the mess hall.

Somehow the cook had gotten a New Year's treat: sweet rice to pound into omochi.

When Meg saw omochi being made in Japan, the sticky ball of rice was put into a carved stone basin. Here in Manzanar, the rice ball was placed inside the bowl carved out of wood.

Two older Japanese men held carved giant hammers, also carved out of wood; the hammers were so big the handles were made from broomsticks. The men wore headbands wrapped tightly around their foreheads. With a smooth tempo, they took turns swinging the hammers down onto the large ball of rice, kneading it with powerful strokes.

It was the third man that Meg couldn't stop watching. He wore a headband too, but he didn't have a hammer. Instead, he used his bare hands to reach into the bowl and turn the lump of rice so it would get pounded evenly. Then he pulled his hands back swiftly, before the next hammer blow landed. First one hammer came down, then the other, then the third man reached in to turn the rice dough. Pound, pound, turn, pound, pound, turn. The tempo increased steadily until Meg could barely see the man's hands slip in and out of the bowl, rolling the lump of rice before the next swing of the hammer came crashing down.

If the hammer were to land in the bowl before the third man got his hands out, the bones in his hands would surely break. But all three men obeyed the rhythm.

A hush fell over the crowd. This was a tradition that took them right back to wherever they had seen rice pounded as children, whether in Japan or in Los Angeles. The men making their omochi were their ojisan, their uncles, whether they were related or not. Even here in a prison camp, the new year of 1943 would be ushered in properly with the traditional Japanese New Year's treat.

By the time the pounding was done, the omochi was firm and elastic. The women took the rounded lump over to the table and divided it into little balls to hand out.

Meg and Deanna each got a piece and then headed out of the mess hall.

Nibbling tiny bits of the sticky rice, making the treat last as long as they could, Deanna walked Meg over to the southwestern corner of the camp to a spot where a thin wild stream flowed down from the Sierras.

The stream came from higher up than they could see, flowing along a rocky creek bed, up and over the stones, spilling and splashing from the corner of Manzanar all the way down to and across the road. Manzanar's back fence stretched over the stream, but nothing could stop the water. Barbed wire didn't mean anything to a mountain stream.

Deanna headed toward a large boulder which split the stream of water. She showed Meg which stones to step on to keep her feet dry and where to put her hand to pull herself up to the top of the huge rock without dropping the omochi.

Sitting together on top, the girls chewed on the last bits of omochi and licked their sticky fingers.

Meg asked the question that had been on her mind.

"How do you do that, anyway?"

"What?"

"Look so pious and holy when you go up to take communion."

"Oh, you noticed that!"

"Yes, Deanna, I noticed."

"Oh, yeah, I know exactly how to do that," Deanna purred.

"What do you mean?" Meg pounced.

"So, when you go up for communion, you kneel like this." Deanna kneeled gracefully on the rock. When she bowed her head, some of her lovely black hair flowed over her shoulders and down along her neck, shadowing her face like a veil. She looked the very image of a pious Virgin Mary.

"Oh, that's so good," breathed Meg. "I could never do that."

"Well, I have been practicing," Deanna said coyly.

Meg giggled. "Yeah, it takes a lot of practice for you to look saintly."

Deanna punched her. "Well, at least I can pull it off."

"I just don't have the hair," Meg said, sighing.

"True," Deanna said with a shrug.

Meg laughed. It was pretty chilly to be sitting on a large rock in the middle of an icy stream fed by a glacier, but Meg and Deanna just didn't care.


## *The Rocks*


The Shinkolobwe rocks were getting pounded worse than sweet rice. Once they left the warehouses in New York City, they traveled by train up to the Port Hope refinery on the Canadian side of Lake Ontario. There, the Canadians had giant grinders that could pulverize the rocks into sand. Then the Shinkolobwe sand was stirred in huge vats with chemicals that dissolved the uranium, dividing it from the waste rock. Then the uranium liquid could be pumped out for drying.

It was a loud and dusty enterprise, this giant maul of rock crushers and ponds of noxious chemicals. Once the liquid uranium was pumped out, it dried in ponds into a yellowish powder called yellowcake. Never again would the Shinkolobwe ore look like rocks. The yellowcake powder could be sealed into metal cans, or mixed with metals into alloys, or combined with chlorine into a uranium salt - whichever formulation the scientists wanted. Then the uranium was on its way again. What was left behind in Canada? Mounds of radioactive dust and ponds of leaching radioactive chemicals along the shore of Lake Ontario.

American physicist Dr. Ernest Lawrence had one of the best ideas for how to separate the U235 from U238. He knew how to use particle accelerators to shoot beams of neutrons toward materials like uranium, but he wondered if a particle accelerator could shoot a beam of uranium instead. And then, if that beam of uranium could be bent, maybe by using magnets to pull the beam into a curve, the U238 would arc in a slightly broader curve because it was just a hint heavier. The U235, being just a shade lighter, could bend in a tighter arc and land in a different receptor for extraction.

A beam of uranium? What? Uranium was a rock, a solid, a powder, a metal! But it could be dissolved into a liquid and then the liquid could be heated in a vacuum to such a dizzying temperature that it could be shot along a thundering pathway as a gas.

Dr. Lawrence named his uranium accelerator a Calutron, after the University of California, where he worked. Because it used electromagnets to propel the ionized uranium speeding along the curved path, this method was called electromagnetic separation. When the material cooled off at the far end of the arc, just the tiniest scrape of metallic residue could be harvested from the landing chamber. It wasn't pure U235, but the ratio of U238 and U235 altered slightly, so Dr. Lawrence called this "enriched" U235. Of course, the enriched U235 could be spun through a Calutron multiple times, and sent through gaseous diffusion filters as well, to pull more and more of the U238 out. How pure was pure enough to support a U235 bomb? That remained to be seen.

Construction began on the first giant Calutron near Knoxville, Tennessee. Hundreds of Tennesseans were hired to build, operate, and maintain the machines. Highly trained chemists would accept the yellowcake salt from Canada, liquify it, vaporize it to searing heat, and shoot it in a stream through the giant machines.

People - most of them young women - were hired to sit on tall stools in front of wall-sized control panels inside the Calutron buildings. They had no idea they were sitting next to shooting beams of uranium gas. They only knew their job was to watch the dials of the electromagnets and keep them steady within the proper range to keep the curve of the beam exactly right. The women learned to predict and play the Calutrons like giant musical instruments to keep the machines running and running and running.

They never saw what went into the machines. They never saw what came out.

# Chapter 11
# Vaporized

*Meg*

It was a cold night when Meg next asked Father to take her in to Manzanar with him. Father was heading back in to attend the evening Manzanar school board meeting to discuss reopening the camp school, which had been closed since the riot.

"Yes, you may come with me. Go get your coat."

The cold wind was a shock when they stepped outside, but the heater in the car worked, and so did the headlights.

The guard at the gate waved them over.

"It's a cold night to be out, Reverend Binnenkerk."

"Is the heat on in the high school?"

"Enough."

"We'll be fine then. You have the harder shift out here." The sentry post was a stone building. It blocked the wind, but it certainly wasn't warm.

Meg got Father's attention. "I'm going to go see if anyone is still in the church." Meg knew that Pastor Wormley had opened the church barracks for students to study on their own until the Manzanar school reopened.

"That's fine, Meg." Father's mind was already on the meeting.

Meg braced herself to walk through the bitter wind. She walked down B Street and then up Fourth Street to Block fifteen, wondering why the streets and buildings in Manzanar couldn't have been given more imaginative names. The tar paper on some of the buildings was flapping against the lathe.

It looked like a lamp was on in the church barracks. Meg hoped the heater was on too. Pulling open the wooden door, she stepped in quickly.

"Hello!" Meg called out.

Deanna was there! So was Pastor Wormley, standing right behind Deanna, squished against her back. He had one arm wrapped around her waist and the other arm stuffed up the front of her sweater. The tails of her shirt were untucked and hanging out. Pastor Wormley's hand was grabbing and rubbing underneath her shirt.

The pastor had been kissing Deanna's neck. He looked up sharply when Meg came in.

Deanna's face looked ghastly. A quick glance around the room told Meg that no one else was present.

I guess I should leave, Meg thought numbly. If Deanna was dating Pastor Wormley, Meg thought, then this was a private moment between them and Meg ought to leave. But how could that be? Meg tried to think. Pastor Wormley was married, wasn't he? And Meg thought he had said he had children.

And he wasn't even likeable. He was sloppy and paunchy and balding. And if for some unfathomable reason Deanna had a crush on him, wouldn't she have told Meg about it?

Meg decided not to leave. Meg pulled her head up two inches, deliberately, and looked straight at Pastor Wormley. Gradually he pulled his hands out of Deanna's blouse. Deanna didn't move a muscle. Deanna stared down at the floor, refusing to meet Meg's eyes.

Wormley looked back at Meg, daring her, taunting her, Meg thought, to stop him from touching Deanna. He cocked his head ever so slightly, but the movement was enough to galvanize Meg into action. Meg picked up her right foot and stepped forward deliberately, and then she lifted the other foot. Each footstep slapped the hollow wooden floor until Meg reached Deanna. Reaching forward, Meg took her friend by the wrist.

"Let's go." Meg pulled. Deanna rocked forward. Wormley's hands fell away.

"Where's your coat?" Meg asked Deanna.

Deanna said nothing. Meg turned, saw Deanna's coat lying over one of the chairs, pulled Deanna over, picked up the coat, and kept moving.

When they were outside, Meg handed Deanna her coat. Deanna was shivering. She thrust her arms in the sleeves and hastily tucked her shirt back into the waistband of her skirt.

Meg wasn't satisfied to let the barracks door fall closed behind them. She pulled the thin wooden door all the way open and then slammed it shut, hoping Wormley would wince at the sound.

Where to go? Meg wasn't about to take Deanna back to the barracks where she lived. Her whole family would be there, along with two other families, their quarters only divided by hanging blankets. That was no place for privacy.

It would be warm in the high school barrack but that was out of the question. The school board meeting was there.

"Where's Mr. Fujii's greenhouse?" Meg demanded. Mr. Fujii was not likely to be there at this hour and he would likely have sheltered his plants from the wind and cold.

Deanna began trudging toward the northern half of the camp. Silently, they pressed through the ugly wind whipping around the barracks until Meg could see the serviceable greenhouse Mr. Fujii had fashioned out of boards and plastic sheeting. Fortunately, the bitter wind had sent everyone else inside so she and Deanna barreled down the empty dirt alley and slipped quietly into the greenhouse.

Inside, breathing in the humid air scented with soil and flowers, Meg turned and faced Deanna. One dim street lamp sent its blurry light through the plastic. Although it had taken several minutes to battle the wind across the length of the camp, Meg still hadn't formulated a single sentence to ask her friend.

"What?" Meg asked. She didn't know what to say beyond that. She couldn't find a second word to form a sentence.

Deanna apparently couldn't find a first word.

Meg sighed and tried again. "He was touching you."

Deanna looked up and met Meg eye to eye.

Ultimately there was just one essential question.

"Did you want him to?"

"He does that," Deanna said. Three words seemed to be all she could muster.

"What do you mean, 'he does that?'" Meg asked.

Meg thought about what Deanna had said, and what she hadn't said. Deanna hadn't said that some kind of unusual accident had forced Pastor Wormley's hands up the front of her shirt. She hadn't said that what Meg had seen was the first time.

Meg was losing patience with the English language. "What do you mean, Deanna? Do you mean he's been doing that?"

"Yes." It was a whisper.

"And?" Meg repeated, "Did you want him to?"

Meg was still trying to get her bearings. She didn't want to intrude. Maybe Deanna was smitten with Pastor Wormley for some mysterious reason. There was no denying Deanna was more self-possessed than Meg, more poised and grown-up, but what Meg saw hadn't looked like affection, much less love.

Deanna was struck dumb again.

Meg tried to find another way, knowing that her words would be awkward at best. At worst, her words would hurt Deanna in ways Meg never intended, but Meg didn't know how to say it without causing harm. "I mean, for one thing, he's married."

"I know!" The words burst from Deanna.

"What are you doing, then?" Meg was louder than she wanted to be.

"It's not me! He tells me to stay to help him clean up and then he waits until everyone is gone."

"Deanna! Then don't go to study hall!"

"It doesn't have to be study hall!" Deanna realized she was nearly yelling, and dropped her voice. "It can be Bible study, or Sunday School. He tells my parents he needs help with the bulletins or with putting away the hymnals."

"How long?"

"Pretty much ever since he got here." A solitary tear spilled down Deanna's cheek, now scarlet with embarrassment.

Suddenly, to Meg, it all became clear. "You didn't want him to."

Deanna found a new voice, fierce, low and husky, like a Russian person rather than a Japanese. "It's not up to me to want or not want. This is just what it's going to be like now."

Something was wrong with the way Deanna was thinking. Deanna thought she had lost some kind of privilege to say yes or no? Why? Because she was a prisoner? Because she was a girl? Because he was a pastor?

Meg tried to clarify by repeating what Deanna had said. "You're saying this is how it's going to be from now on."

"Yes." Deanna glared at Meg, like it was obvious. "Every time I walk to school. Even when I walk to church," she said with extra emphasis.

Meg decided to push. "What do you mean? You think anyone can decide whether to touch you? A pastor, too?"

Deanna looked at Meg. "Apparently yes."

"Apparently no!" Meg blurted.

"Yes, they do, Meg." Deanna stepped right into Meg's face. "One minute I can see the boys thinking about who gets to have me, like they are negotiating with each other. And then the next minute it's like anyone can, and they don't even have to debate it."

"But if you don't want to …" Meg's voice trailed off. What did she know? Her chest was as flat as Walter's. Maybe it was inevitable to become public property for leering and grabbing. Beyond inevitable, maybe it was normal.

Meg had seen the way Yasuo looked at Deanna, the hungry beam of his attention on her. Meg had watched Deanna smile and swing her hair, seemingly confident to be the target of his attention.

"No. That's not right," Meg hissed.

A new idea hit Meg like a hammer hitting the omochi. When the boys stared at Deanna, and teased her and flirted with her, it wasn't a compliment. It was a threat.

Now Meg was the one who couldn't speak.

Deanna looked at her agonizingly.

"Meg! What if my parents find out? They respect Pastor Wormley. He's not even Japanese!"

"Don't you think they'll be more mad at him than you?"

"He is a minister!" Deanna hissed. "They can't be mad at him. And he can come and go from this camp as he pleases. He can come in whenever he wants and leave whenever he wants."

Deanna's voice dropped about an octave: "I know what he is. I know he's just a man who's cheating on his wife. I know he'll just spend a few months here and then just go on somewhere else."

Meg's eyes widened. "Cheating? What do you mean? Do you mean you're actually having …? I mean … going to bed with him?"

"No!" Deanna cried, stamping her foot. The tears were flowing out of her eyes now but, curiously, they stopped and pooled halfway down her cheek, leaving a soggy ridge. Even her silken hair was looking stricken, with little stray ends poking away from her cheeks in distress.

"No!" Deanna yelled again. "But what's to stop him?"

"You! You stop him!" Meg couldn't fathom a scenario in which what Deanna wanted meant nothing. This was Deanna. She could always find a way to get what she wanted.

"I can't," Deanna hazarded, deflated.

Meg couldn't hear any more. "I don't think that's right."

Deanna looked at Meg, arms crossed over her chest.

Another horrible thought crossed Meg's mind. "He might be doing that to other girls, too."

Deanna looked a little surprised. "That's true," she said.

"I know what to do." Meg announced.

"No, Meg. You are not going to tell your father."

"No, no," Meg said. "Not that. But first, we're never going to call him 'pastor' again."

"OK."

"And there's something else," Meg said.

"What?" Deanna said warily. It sounded to her like a Meg-shaped disaster was in the works.

Meg leaned over to her friend and whispered one word, "Tricycles."

## *The Rocks*

Assuming the vaporized beams of uranium could separate U235 from U238, the next question was how to turn the U235 into a weapon.

The first step was to figure out exactly how much fissionable material like U235 was needed to make a bomb powerful enough to level a city. The way the U235 was arranged could make a difference, too. If the U235 was shaped into a sphere - like a cannon ball - it was more likely that neutrons would stay close to the fissile material rather than skipping away. The scientists decided that to consume the entire mass of U235 very quickly, the U235 would have to be shaped into an extremely heavy cannon ball.

Of course, it had to be transportable, too. The scientists didn't want it to explode prematurely and they didn't want it to release its energy in a slow fizzle of radiation. They needed to configure the U235 so it could be carried safely across the country and across the ocean, completely inert, before being dropped on the target in Germany.

That meant the initiator which would start the flow of neutrons had to be kept apart from the U235 until after the bomb was dropped from an airplane.

They had already chosen polonium as the initiator. Polonium was an element that spewed neutrons. A Hungarian radiochemist named Dr. Elizabeth Rona was the best in the world at extracting polonium through a meticulous process of controlled radioactive decay.

Before the war, Dr. Rona had worked with Dr. Hahn and Dr. Meitner in Germany and Dr. Irène Joliot-Curie in France. She knew everything they knew, and more, about how to extract and handle polonium. She gladly supplied polonium to the American bomb project and went one step further, teaching the Americans her methods without charge.

Gradually, the plan for a U235 bomb came together. The metallic U235 would be shaped into a hollow sphere and held in place at one end of the muzzle of a very large and heavy gun. The polonium catalyst would be nestled inside the hollow core of the U235 cannon ball. But it wouldn't be a complete sphere; it would have a wedge missing. The missing wedge of U235 would be held in place at the other the other end of the muzzle, with an explosive detonator behind it. Keeping the U235 divided into two sub-critical masses would keep the chain reaction at bay.

When the detonator went off, the U235 bullet would shoot down the muzzle into the U235 sphere, igniting the polonium trigger, and setting the chain reaction ablaze. The spherical design would keep freed neutrons close to support an exponential chain reaction, so the U235 would all be consumed nearly instantaneously in a single giant explosion.

A bomb like this could be carried in parts on a ship and then assembled and loaded onto the bay of an airplane. The detonation could be set to fire while the bomb was falling through the air, so it would explode over the chosen city in Germany while the plane sped away to safety.

There certainly wasn't any U235 to spare for a trial run, but even in 1943, the scientists had tested enough of the components to know a bomb like this could work. Now everything depended on those giant Calutrons in Tennessee churning out a critical mass of enriched U235. It looked like about a hundred pounds of enriched U235 would be needed for a single bomb. That would take at least a year.

# Chapter 12
# Taking the Fight to the Enemy

*Meg*

Meg slipped out of church between the early service and Sunday School to help Deanna undergo a minor but significant transformation. Her long gleaming black hair was caught up in two long braids sticking out from the sides of her head. No more was Deanna the smooth Madonna filled with gentle piety, or the sultry queen of the mess hall. Now Deanna looked like a plucky little gal from a storybook, like someone who ought to have freckles painted on her nose and jaunty ribbons tied at the ends of her braids.

Meg and Deanna ran between the barracks, breathlessly sweeping into Block 15 just as Sunday School was wrapping up. As expected, the children were stacking up the nursery toys and pulling on their mother's kimonos, ready to leave. Deanna and Meg each grabbed a tricycle and began to pedal madly around the back of the room.

"Let's go outside," Meg hollered. The altar guild ladies putting away the hymnals looked up, frowning.

"We need more room to ride!" Deanna yelled, just as Father stepped out of the vestments' room.

Meg and Deanna carried the tricycles clattering down the wooden steps and lined them up for an impromptu tricycle race up the long dirt avenue.

Wormley was standing at the base of the stairs, shaking hands with departing parishioners. Out of the corner of her eye, Meg could see him purse his lips.

"Ichi, Ni, San, Go!" yelled Meg, much too loudly. Then she and Deanna were off on the child-size tricycles, knees pumping up almost up to their chins. Deanna swerved suddenly to avoid a fist-sized rock. One of her back wheels arched and lifted, threatening the stability of the trike, but Deanna kept pedaling and the wheel fell back to the ground with a smack.

Ahead of them, a couple of teenaged boys were slouched against a barrack wall, hands in pockets, affecting their best Clark Gable.

"Hey!" Deanna yelled over to them. "Come to the middle. We need a turnaround post to steer around."

She needn't have yelled. There wasn't any rush. The pace of the tricycles was so slow that time seemed to stretch into lazy minutes as they pedaled ferociously inch by inch toward in front of the boys.

Not that either boy responded to Deanna's demand anyway. Incredulous, they watched as the girls drove past, all pretense of daintiness abandoned.

Deanna tried to turn first, pulling the handlebars sharply to the left, but that just pressed the left handle into her rib cage. "We'll have to get off to turn," she yelled over her shoulder.

It was wholly unnecessary for Deanna to raise her voice with Meg a scant foot away, but Deanna yelled as if gale force winds were swirling around them. The girls untangled themselves from the tricycles, picked up the trikes, and placed them down on a new starting line.

Meg darted ahead and put hers down a couple of feet ahead of Deanna's.

"No fair!" Deanna yelled and put her head down, pedaling like a furious hamster.

Meg broke into laughter and couldn't stop. Some little spit of Manzanar grit kicked up into her eye as Deanna passed her. Meg's eye started to water, but she refused to allow herself the time to wipe her eye. She slid her legs under the handlebars, angled her knees out, squeezed her feet onto the pedals and headed out after Deanna.

They inched their way back to Block 15. The few remaining Japanese parishioners ignored them studiously. Miss Moroni, standing next to Wormley, looked angry. Father emerged from the church and stood at the top of the steps.

"I win! I win!" hollered Deanna, pulling herself off the tricycle with admirable grace right at the base of the church steps.

"Whee!" yelled Meg, sticking both legs out in front of her to glide to a stop, lurching forward when her trike hit a small rock.

"Orokana," stated one of deacons, grabbing his wide-eyed child by the hand and walking stiffly away.

Yes, they were being frivolous, headstrong children, thought Meg. That was exactly the goal. Mission accomplished.

"Gomen'nasai!" Deanna called out after him, cheerfully begging his pardon. "Do you need help getting off the bike, Meg?"

"I think I do!" Meg dissolved into laughter. She couldn't get her left knee out from under the handlebars.

"Let me help," suggested Deanna, and began turning the handlebars to trap Meg further into the tricycle, sending Meg into snorting giggles.

"Enough," Meg begged for relief, and finally unfolded herself from the tricycle.

"Good race," Deanna said with the hearty congratulation of a radio announcer.

"Good race," Meg echoed, attempting a severe facial expression to squelch her laughter.

The girls carried the tricycles back into the church and parked them in the line along the back wall with the blocks and dolls. Clomping down the stairs, Deanna called out sweetly to those gathered around the stairs, "Sayonara!"

The girls' hands found each other as they walked east toward the road.

"We are not running away," Deanna muttered through gritted smiling teeth.

"Nope, we're just walking," agreed Meg as they swung their clasped hands between them, gliding away from the church barracks. Meg exaggerated her stride, sliding one foot forward after the other in long sweeps, the complete opposite of mincing Japanese geisha steps. Deanna laughed and yanked on Meg's arm, pulling Meg back to a normal stride.

Out of the corner of her eye, Meg could see Wormley push through the departing parishioners and slink back into the barracks.

It was the most ordinary thing in the world for the two girls to walk, holding hands, down the dusty pathway as the sun rose higher and higher over the Inyo Range and sent its rays sparkling down on them.

## *The Rocks*

While Meg reminded Wormley that she and Deanna were still actually children, Dr. Oppenheimer had to remind General Groves that the workers in Los Alamos were scientists, not soldiers.

If General Groves had his way, everyone in Los Alamos would have been commissioned into service, given ranks, a strict chain of command, military orders, and military discipline.

But Dr. Oppenheimer prevailed. Yes, the scientists were setting their individual careers aside. Yes, they agreed not to publish, even though publishing their discoveries would no doubt have led to admiration, fame, job offers and tenure at the world's most renowned universities. But ultimately, they wanted to remain scientists - on loan only to the U.S. government.

Ironically, drawing a circle of silence among the experts gathered in Los Alamos gave them more intellectual freedom than they had ever known. They didn't need to publish in journals to share their findings because their colleagues were living right next door. They could discuss their work during the day in the laboratory and meet in the evenings to talk some more. They could chat during Sunday hikes, horseback rides and ski trips to the mountains around Santa Fe. What's more, these were physicists sharing with chemists, sharing with metallurgists, sharing with mathematicians. The Los Alamos laboratory became the most cohesive scientific collaboration the world had ever seen.

Dr. Oppenheimer created that atmosphere of curiosity and urgency. The laboratory opened with a series of evening lectures on their goal and what was known so far. Then, during the day, they sought to advance that knowledge, step by step.

# Chapter 13
# Secrets

*Meg*

Father was frowning at Meg. She was keeping a secret from him, and he didn't approve. Father stood still, radiating patient equanimity, using Walter's trick to get Meg to talk. Meg stood before him, still wearing her overcoat, shifting her weight from one foot to the other. Father wanted an explanation for her behavior with the tricycles.

To his credit, Father had waited until they had loaded up the car, waved at the guard at the Manzanar gate, and driven all the way back to Independence. Meg had rolled down the car window a crack, pretending to be overly warm, and spent the ride looking out the window, saying nothing.

Now apparently Father would wait no more. He stood still, looking steadily at Meg, waiting for her to explain herself.

From the kitchen, Meg could hear Mother and Amy. They were sitting together in the over-stuffed chair, reading the same book over and over. As soon as Mother turned the last page, Amy would grab the book and turn it over to the front cover. That was her way of demanding that Mother read it again.

Meg could hear Walter slam the door to the back porch, whistling as he went out to his shed.

If Meg wanted to be allowed to go back in to Manzanar, and continue to protect Deanna, this was the moment she had to figure out what to say to her father.

On the one hand, Father needed to know what kind of person Wormley was. On the other hand, Deanna didn't want Meg to tell, and especially not to tell Father.

As Meg tried to decide what to do, a third consideration wormed through her mind. Father wasn't just Wormley's co-worker. Father was Deanna's chaplain. He was supposed to guide and protect her. On the other hand, if Deanna had wanted to confide in him as her pastor, wouldn't she have done so herself?

Meg had been trained her whole life not to do anything that would reflect badly on her Father's ministry. "Never be a stumbling block to one who wants to believe," Father had gravely instructed them. Now, Meg had deliberately acted silly in front of the whole church.

But if anyone was a stumbling block, wasn't it Wormley? Wasn't it Wormley who was getting in the way of Deanna's belief? Maybe Meg had done exactly what a good Christian daughter should do under the circumstances.

Meg crossed her arms stubbornly.

The truth was that Deanna hadn't chosen to confide in either Father or Meg. Meg had been so quick to grab Deanna away from Wormley, and push her out the door, and tell her what to do, that she hadn't taken the time to let that sorrow sink in. I've become American, Meg thought with surprise. A Japanese person would have demurred and deferred. Meg hadn't. Well, good, Meg thought. Someone had to do something.

Still Father waited. Could she out wait him? Staring at the sink, and then at the ice box, Meg waited for Father to shrug and assume that Meg would confide in him when she was good and ready. But he didn't.

Ultimately, Meg had to speak.

"Wormley was touching Deanna on her body, where he shouldn't have." There. The words were out. Meg was drenched with regret. She had broken her word to her only friend.

"This is what she told you?"

Meg had never heard Father speak so softly in her entire life.

"No, I saw it." Was Father suggesting that Deanna's word couldn't be trusted? Meg wasn't going to tolerate any possibility that Father wouldn't believe her.

Father looked at her sharply.

"And I promised her I wouldn't tell you." The words came out in a rush.

Father was still trying to understand. "So, with the tricycles, that's what you decided to do?"

"Yes."

Now Meg's eyes were brimming with tears. She blinked them away fiercely. Meg had been so proud of fighting back. To Meg's mind, Operation Tricycle had been brilliant. All they had to do was remind Wormley by behaving so childishly, so unpredictably, that they would do what they chose, not what he chose. It would show him that Deanna wouldn't be cowed and Meg wouldn't either.

Father lowered his chin slightly. "Meg, Deanna's a seductive girl."

Instantly, Meg was furious. Her arms pulled apart and her hands landed on her hips. Her right foot stamped, actually stamped, on the floor. Was Father going to take Wormley's side?

"Saying that is wrapping a millstone around her neck," Meg hissed.

Father couldn't possibly understand what Meg meant. Meg hardly knew what she meant.

"You don't toss her into the sea like that," Meg accused, but her words were mixed up. She was being confusing just when she wanted to be clear. There was no sea anywhere nearby. They were thousands of miles from Japan. Meg knew her words didn't make sense to Father.

Now Meg could hear Mother listening, holding Amy still. Meg stamped the floor again.

Father's eyes widened.

"Meg, I realize that Deanna is your friend ..." Father began.

Yes, that was exactly it. Finally, Meg had a friend and no one was going to hurt her or twist her around just because she was trapped in a camp, especially not a person who pretended to be a minister. It was wrong and Meg wasn't going to allow it.

"Yes, Deanna is my friend," Meg said, lifting her head.

Meg was confused, and she was tired. A headache circled her head, pounding in from all directions. In the end, Meg didn't know what to do about Wormley, to make him stop taking liberties with Deanna, or any other girl.

Meg was sure of a couple of things, though. The church was Father's responsibility. Now that Father knew what Wormley was doing, it was Father's duty to deal with him. Meg only wanted safety for the girls, all those pearl divers holding in their breath while the ocean closed in.

"Alright," Father said, watching the confusion and sorrow flicker over his daughter's face.

Meg felt her mother relax. Mother picked up Amy's book again.

Meg didn't know how much Father truly saw, how much he understood. Meg stuck her hands in the pockets of her coat, reaching into the corners of the pocket. Meg realized she was feeling for the tiny pebble she had put in the pocket way back in Zeeland. Where was it? Meg ran her fingers along the seam at the bottom of each pocket. She turned away from Father so she could concentrate. It was obvious the pebble was missing. It had either fallen out or Mother had found it before putting the coat in the wash. If Meg wanted to, she could certainly find a new pebble, but this one was gone. Meg shrugged out of her coat and walked over to the front door to hang it up.

## The Rocks

Spilling secrets has consequences, but keeping secrets does, too. What do you think happened when all the most famous scientists in America disappeared, simply evaporating from the universities and laboratories? No longer publishing articles. No longer giving interviews. No longer presenting at conferences.

They had stopped for good reason, to make sure their inventions didn't end up in the wrong hands. But that absence of communication was telling, too.

These people had been a pretty chatty bunch before the war. Dr. Szilárd knew just about everyone in the global physics community. So did Dr. Fermi. So did Dr. Oppenheimer. Now, their silence broadcasted to everyone who knew how to listen that something was up in the United States of America. The silence emanating from the U.S. meant the Americans were, without a doubt, working on a bomb.

How strange that not announcing the bomb project was tantamount to announcing a bomb project. The question was, what could any of the other countries do about it?

# Chapter 14
# Spontaneous Fission

*Meg*

Meg was ready - more than ready - for Father to do something with the information she had shared with him about Wormley.

Meg sat on the porch steps of their little house in Independence, watching Amy. Amy had to be monitored constantly. She had a tendency to put anything and everything in her mouth. And now that she was starting to pull herself up, she could reach items the family thought were out of her reach.

Meg was fussing with her boots. She had just succeeded in getting one boot on when the rest of the family emerged from the house. They were heading for church in Manzanar. Meg had been worried that Father wouldn't let her go back into Manzanar with him, but this Sunday the whole family was going.

Meg tucked the other boot under her arm and hopped over to Amy. There was something suspicious in Amy's hand. Meg unfolded Amy fingers. Four pebbles.

"No, Amy," Meg said, "you can't have these."

Amy immediately launched into wails and clenched her chubby hand shut. Meg peeled her thumb and fingers open and placed the pebbles up on the porch railing.

"Come on," Meg said, lifting Amy into her arms without dropping the boot. Meg limped toward the car. She would put on her second boot in the car.

They would just have to listen to Amy screaming the whole way.

"Shigataganai," Meg muttered to herself. It couldn't be helped. The whole Owens Valley was covered with pebbles. Amy was bound to pick up some of them.

Amy cried the whole way to the camp. Mother spoke sharply to Amy as they pulled through the gate. Amy stopped crying and stuffed three of her little fingers inside her mouth. Father parked next to the camp office and they walked to the church together.

Stepping inside, Meg was glad to see that Wormley wasn't there, but just then he stepped out of the vestments' room.

"Why is he still here?" Meg whispered to Mother.

"Shh," Mother said. "Here," Mother continued, "take your sister."

Dumbly, Meg took Amy and went to sit down.

The words of the service were like dust for Meg. There was Wormley, going through the motions, near the altar, with her father. The whole idea of it was unacceptable.

Meg looked around the congregation. Deanna's parents were there, but no Deanna.

As soon as the final benediction was offered, Meg whispered to Walter, "Watch Amy," and she slipped through the chairs and out the barrack door without even asking permission.

Meg thought it unlikely that Deanna would be at home; if she had been there, her parents would have made her come to church.

Meg peeked into Mr. Fujii's greenhouse. Mr. Fujii was there, clipping and trimming his plants, but Deanna wasn't.

Meg pulled her coat tighter around her chest. She wondered if she could find the way back to the large boulder in the stream. Using the mountains as her guide, Meg headed south to the edge of the camp. She found the stream and followed it west. The water was wild today. Meg stepped through the leaves, wet and slimy from freeze and thaw, and climbed up on the rock. The water was jumping and pushing its way east, as if fighting other droplets to slide first over the rocks.

The water was rushing, either away from or toward something, but in either event, Deanna wasn't there. Meg slid off the rock, accidentally dunking her foot in the biting cold water, and walked alongside the stream until it crossed back under the camp fence. Meg turned back into camp. She followed the front road, unsure about where to go next, when she saw Frank and his friends at the makeshift basketball court. That's where Deanna was.

Someone had built a wooden bench and placed it alongside the court. Meg sat down, grateful to rest her pinched feet.

The court was crowded with more than five players on a side. It looked like Deanna was the only girl playing. She was wearing the same kind of pants as the boys, with her dark hair pulled up in a rubber band.

Frank had possession of the ball. He tossed it to one of the boys, but Deanna stole it and took a shot from mid-court. The ball hit the rim and rolled in. By the time it fell, Deanna was already hoofing backwards to set up the defense. Arms out, she yelled for the defensive positions. A pass. Her opponent tried to send the shot just left of her hands. Deanna dove and blocked the shot, grabbing the ball while keeping her right leg planted. Deanna passed the ball to her brother, then trekked back across the court while he dribbled next to her. Deanna diverted to the side line. Frank planted his feet and looked around for his team.

"I'm open," Deanna called. Frank shrugged and passed her the ball. Deanna shot again, missed, snagged the rebound, and shot again, sinking the ball.

As Meg watched, the game changed. Now the only goal was to pass to Deanna as often as possible. Everyone on Frank's team fell into line. If the team couldn't steal it for her, Deanna charged at her opponents, shoved through their lines, and grabbed the ball. There was no point in calling a foul.

Catch and pass to Deanna. Shoot. Catch and pass to Deanna. Steal and pass to Deanna. Shoot. Shoot. Shoot. Sometimes Deanna made the basket. Sometimes she missed. No one was keeping score anyway.

A couple of the boys stopped running and stood in the back-court, breathing hard. One by one, the boys pulled back. Eventually they all stepped off the court, lined up along the perimeter with only Frank, Deanna, and one other boy left at the basket.

The pace was relentless. The boy Meg barely recognized stayed under the basket, passing each shot to Frank, who bulleted it over to Deanna, who jumped and slammed and flung the ball toward the basket. As soon as the ball was out of her hands, Deanna leaped to another part of the court, eyes on Frank, ready to take the next shot.

Who would know when the game was over? Frank was the only one who could call it, Meg thought. If Frank hadn't been there, the boys probably wouldn't have let Deanna play at all. Now Frank would have to find a way to bring it to an end.

Meg felt someone slide onto the bench next to her. It was Walter.

"Hey," Meg said.

Meg wasn't typically interested in sports, but, then again, what was happening on the court wasn't sport. It was about determination, necessity, unstoppability.

The clutch of boys along the sidelines formed a thin line blocking the court from the casual viewer. This wasn't a casual game and it wasn't the business of any adults walking by.

Deanna caught a toe on a small rock and staggered but did not fall. Frank threw a hard pass her way. It hit her in the belly but she got control over it.

Frank loped underneath the hoop, taking the other boy's place. Now that boy was out, too. Deanna took the shot, Frank caught it, and threw it back to her. She took another shot. Through the hoop. Down to Frank and pass to Deanna. Shoot. Pass. Shoot.

Now that only the two of them were on the court, Deanna stopped playing all the angles and picked a position directly in front of Frank. They were carving a triangle through the air, from Deanna's hands up to the plywood backboard, down through the hoop into Frank's hands, across from Frank's hands to Deanna's.

Without notice, without any bell or signal, Frank caught the ball and tucked it under his arm. "That's it."

All of the spectators swayed back slightly, expecting the ball to come out of Frank's hands, but he held onto it.

Deanna dodged back and forth, feigning, but Frank wouldn't pass it to her. Instead, he reached all the way back, the ball cradled in one hand, and threw the ball in a high arc over Deanna, over the spectators, over Manzanar's main dirt road, where it bounced harmlessly in the gutter and rolled to the wall of the first barrack.

Frank lifted the edge of his shirt to wipe the sweat from his face. Deanna simply spun and walked away.

Suddenly, Meg felt exposed. She didn't belong in this place after all, with Deanna and Frank. Meg had wanted to have a best friend for a long time, but having a friend meant being a friend, and that was turning out to be harder than she had thought. Meg didn't know if she should follow Deanna or not. Had Deanna even noticed she was there? Probably not.

"Mother is looking for you," Walter said quietly. "It's time to go."

It was nice of Walter to have waited.

"Ok," Meg said. She and Walter stood up and stepped over the bench. They headed over to the gate where the car was parked. Mother was there, with Amy. Father was nowhere in sight. They waited for him together.

### The Rocks

No matter how the scientists tried to configure it, a gun-type assembly didn't work for the plutonium. Plutonium was just too fickle. Keeping sub-critical masses apart wasn't enough to keep a chain reaction at bay. The plutonium would fissile spontaneously and spew neutrons everywhere. For one thing, that wasn't safe. For another, it wasn't a bomb.

Like Deanna playing basketball, plutonium broke the rules.

Instead of exploding out, plutonium needed a bomb design where it would explode in. An inward explosion would squish all the fleeing neutrons right back into the plutonium, so the chain reaction would burst all the plutonium at once and generate a massive slam of heat, a shock wave and an immense explosion of radiation.

It was one thing to conceive of a design like this, another thing altogether to make it work. The plutonium could be shaped into a small heavy ball, but then it would need to be wrapped in a shell of explosives that would all ignite at exactly the same instant. If the explosives weren't perfectly synchronized to go off simultaneously, the plutonium would bulge out one side or the other and the neutrons would spew out instead of in. Perfectly spherical inward compression was the goal. The plutonium needed to collapse in, and then explode out. Los Alamos engineers started working on a design like a soccer ball, with curved lens of explosives fitting together in a sphere, leaving a hollow nook inside for the precious plutonium core.

# Chapter 15
# Loyalty

*Meg*

Just like the engineers in Los Alamos, Meg realized she needed a new tactic.

Back at home in Independence, Meg helped Mother finish preparing Sunday dinner. After dinner, she cleared the table. She washed the dishes. She put Amy down for her nap. She waited until after Father had his Sunday afternoon nap.

Then, Meg decided the time had come.

She wanted to send up a quick prayer, but she didn't know to whom to send it. For some reason, this prayer couldn't go to God the Father. One of Meg's favorite Christmas carols was The Friendly Beasts, about Jesus our Brother. That was who got this prayer, her brother

Jesus. He was sort of like her brother Walter, only older. Meg winged her prayer, not up to God, but over to Jesus, her brother.

Meg had her coat and boots on already. "Father, will you go for a walk with me, please?"

Ever so slowly, Father put on his rubber galoshes, coat, hat and gloves. They closed the front door behind them and walked north up the sidewalk, away from the town.

Looking straight ahead, Meg asked, "Why is Wormley still here?" It felt like a risk not to use the title in front of his name, but Meg had sworn never to call him pastor again.

"Well, Meg," Father said slowly, "Dale Wormley still has a couple of months on this assignment."

Meg noticed that Father didn't called him pastor either.

"His assignment is over," Meg said bluntly.

"This is not something I can discuss with you." Father took a few steps forward. "But I will say that Director Merritt did re-assign him to housing outside the camp. He won't be in camp in the evenings unless there is a church activity."

Meg appreciated that Father was talking with her like a grown-up, calling the camp director by his full name. Maybe Father was just indulging her, but Meg didn't care. She felt like she was in a play, saying her lines.

"That's not good enough," Meg said. Moving Wormley out of camp meant they probably gave him a car. It was like giving him a reward.

"And he better not live in Independence," Meg declared.

"No," Father said slowly. "He found a room in Lone Pine."

Meg had planned her next step before broaching the topic with Father. "Here's what's going to happen." Meg took a deep breath. "From now on, the girls in church are going to sit together in the front row, every Sunday, every Bible Study, every time."

Father was completely floored. "Why would they do that?"

"Because Deanna and I are going to tell them."

"Tell them what?"

"Tell them to watch out for Wormley. Tell them what he does to girls. So he knows the jig is up."

"How will Dale be able to minister to any of them, then?" Father's mouth didn't close.

Meg just looked up at her father. Of course, Wormley couldn't minister to them. Of course, he wasn't ministering to them. He was a total fraud.

"They have to be warned, don't they?" Meg continued, relentless. "I mean, Deanna's parents need to know, too, right?"

"How is he expected to do his work after that?" Father was still shocked.

"Exactly."

"I don't think ...," Father paused then said. "It was an indiscretion on his part."

"Are you saying you didn't tell the other girls so they would know about him?" Meg asked.

"Of course not," Father said. "That would be a breach of confidentiality. And I'm sure Deanna would not want you spreading this gossip."

"How can you be up in front of the church with him? How can he give communion?" The idea of Wormley placing a communion wafer into anyone's open mouth made Meg shudder.

Father looked distinctly uncomfortable, like he was betraying a confidence. "I spoke with Dale and told him to be more circumspect."

"Father, the problem with the belt of truth is that you can't just take it off. You can't just put it on and then take it off."

Father's face went blank and then he frowned, but it didn't seem as though the frown was for her.

Father had taught them the Bible verses about putting on the armor of God and wearing the belt of truth. It wasn't Meg's fault that her armor was a red tricycle.

"Meg, this really isn't your concern." Father tried to be firm.

Meg's eyes filled with tears. She refused to let them spill over and freeze on her cheeks.

It could have been any girl in that camp. It could be more girls. There was no particular reason to believe that Deanna was Wormley's only teenaged conquest.

"He made it my business when he picked on Deanna," Meg said, feeling like a 1920's gangster, like Al Capone.

Imagine if Meg hadn't met Deanna that day. Imagine if Father had been assigned to a different camp. Who would be there then, to give Wormley the shove he deserved?

"I can't fault your loyalty," Father admitted.

To whom are you loyal? Meg wondered silently. Why wouldn't you boot Wormley back to wherever he came from?

"That's all I wanted to say," Meg said stiffly, and pivoted to head home, leaving Father standing on the sidewalk. Loyalty couldn't be bought or sold. It was owned and it was owed, and in Meg's opinion, Father's loyalty was owed to her and to Deanna. Deanna might have thought that telling Father was a breach of loyalty, but for Meg, getting Father to do something was exactly what loyalty commanded.

## *The Rocks*

For the scientists, the question of loyalty wasn't just about which country to work for, but whether or not to work on a bomb at all. For almost all of them, this was an easy question to answer. The Nazi army had to be stopped. Germany was most likely working on a nuclear bomb, too, and that was that. The Americans had to work as fast as they could, as hard as they could, as smart as they could, to be first to the bomb.

At least one scientist sized things up differently, and refused to work on a bomb. Can you guess who she was?

Dr. Hahn's mentor and former laboratory partner Dr. Lise Meitner could have made it to the United States. She was safe in neutral Sweden, but she wasn't particularly happy there. She didn't have a great laboratory to work in. She didn't even have a laboratory assistant. She hated the war and the Nazis.

And the Americans invited her. They would have welcomed her. But Dr. Meitner refused. Even though war was raging around her, even though the Fascist movement threatened the whole continent of Europe, even though the Russians were now making moves of their own into Europe, Dr. Meitner said simply, "I will have nothing to do with a bomb."

Was that loyalty? Or disloyalty?

# Chapter 16
# More About Loyalty

*Meg*

Meg pulled her coat tighter around her as she walked through the guard gate at Manzanar. Father dropped her off and head on south to Lone Pine, instructing her to stay with Miss Moroni until he got back. Today, he was picking up the new seminarian assigned to Manzanar. Wormley's replacement. That was a bit of good news on this otherwise bitterly cold day.

"Good morning, Miss Moroni," Meg said cheerfully, stepping into the administration building.

Miss Moroni didn't even look up from whatever she was doing at the giant desk.

"Miss Moroni?" Meg asked.

"I certainly don't have time to talk with the likes of you," the tiny woman declared, spinning her chair around on its casters to pull something from a file cabinet behind her.

"I'm so sorry," Meg stammered. What had she done to get on the wrong side of Miss Moroni? "I just wanted to let you know that I'm here and my father will be along shortly."

"Why you are here, I have no idea. Far beyond your place."

"I see," Meg said softly, tiptoeing back out of the administration building. Perhaps Miss Moroni was one of those people who were only sweet when the boss was around. In any event, Meg didn't want to give her any opportunity to complain about Meg being allowed in Manzanar.

It was so cold that Meg expected most of the residents to be inside. The heaters in their barracks put out a decent amount of warmth if they hovered close by and vented the smoke properly. To Meg's surprise, though, the prison town of Manzanar seemed to be in something of a hubbub. Usually somber Japanese-Americans were gathered in clumps, discussing something. What it was Meg couldn't tell; conversations halted when she passed by. They nodded toward her, but waited until she passed to resume their discussion.

The best place to find out what was going on, Meg thought, was the mess hall.

Meg's coat was too thin for the dusty Manzanar grit blowing in the winter wind, and she could feel the sand working into her thin shoes, but she persisted, making the familiar turns between the barracks. Sure enough, there were groups of Japanese-Americans gathered on the long boards that provided steps up into the hall. Deanna's brother Frank was there with his father and some of the other older men.

Their discussion quieted, but did not fully abate as Meg made her way through the dining hall. To the older issei generation in Manzanar, Meg was guygen, a stranger, but she was also the daughter of a Protestant chaplain, and she spoke Japanese. She and Walter weren't children of Manzanar, but maybe they were seen as some kind of distant relative, twice or thrice removed. Would Frank tell her what the hubbub was about?

"What's going on, Frank?" Meg asked. "And where's Deanna?"

"She's somewhere around here." Frank answered the second question but not the first.

Meg was tempted to roll her eyes. Obviously, Deanna would be around somewhere; it was a prison camp and she wasn't allowed out. But Meg managed to control her eyeballs. After all, Frank didn't even have to speak to her. Just to have Deanna's older brother acknowledge her, and address her, was a show of respect.

"Deanna might be in the park," Mr. Matsumoto said quietly.

Meg's eyes fell on the documents they each were holding. Now that she noticed it, she noticed that everyone seemed to be holding one. It seemed impolite to ask what it was, but Meg's curiosity was sparked. Clearly, this was what everyone was discussing.

"Can I help with something?" That was Meg's attempt at tact.

Frank sighed. He handed the document to her.

"What is it?"

"An oath," Frank stated briefly.

"What for?"

"We have to declare that we're loyal to the U.S."

"OK." There must have been more to it than that, to cause so much consternation.

Frank took the document back and turned away. Apparently, that was all Meg was going to get to learn. Maybe Deanna would tell her more, if she could find her.

Peace Park was on the other side of the camp, toward the orchard. Meg wrapped her coat around her as tightly as she could, and braced herself for a windy walk across Manzanar.

The park was fairly barren. Long water pipes had been laid on the ground to carry sweet cold water down from the mountains. The water pipes dumped into large basins lined with cement, arranged in a graceful curve with adjoining pipes so that one basin drained or overflowed into the next, creating a pathway of small ponds and waterfalls. Walkways of crushed stone wound around the ponds and trees and led to a wooden gazebo. There was even an arched bridge of wood planks and polished branches spanning over one of the spillways where the ponds connected.

The still areas of water supported aquatic plants with lily pads, and reeds and flower beds had already been planted along the edges. Meg wondered if someday, someone would be able to find red and white koi fish to live in the ponds.

Meg knew it wasn't that the families loved Manzanar so much they wanted to memorialize it with a park. Rather, the prisoners wanted to make their confinement as habitable as they could. Here in this park they could transport themselves to a different place, mentally if not physically.

Mr. Fujii was there, inspecting some of the trees for frost damage.

"Ohiogozaimus," Meg greeted him with a polite bow. He nodded back. Deanna was nowhere in sight. Meg debated between heading further north or back toward the basketball court.

In the end, she did neither. She wandered back the way she had come, then headed west up the central Manzanar pathway toward the cemetery.

On her right was the judo pavilion. That's where Meg finally spotted Deanna. The boys' classes were over for the day, but it looked like Deanna was holding an impromptu judo class for little girls.

They were gathered on a corner of the woven mat. Deanna was surrounded by a cluster of five and six-year-olds. The girls were trying to be serious and concentrate, like Deanna was, but hidden giggles bubbled through.

One by one, Deanna showed each little girl the stance, legs spread wide, then Deanna hooked one leg in front, leaned into the girl, and gracefully flipped her over onto her back on the mat.

No matter how many times they saw it happen before it was their turn, each little girl looked up in shock and amazement to find themselves suddenly back down on the mat. Then each girl scrambled up and begged for another turn.

Meg stepped over to one of the pillars to watch Deanna's class.

When each girl had had several turns, Deanna chose the smallest of them to come forward. Deanna assumed the broad-legged stance and showed the girl where to place her leg and how to lean her body weight into Deanna's body, pushing her ever so slightly off balance, and causing Deanna to roll in a controlled slow motion over the girl's back and falling onto the mat. Suddenly, it was Deanna who was down on the mat. The tiny girl was left standing, shouting with the thrill of her victory.

Now all the girls pressed around Deanna, wanting their turn to flip the teacher. They pulled Deanna up to her feet and closed a circle around her, pulling her by the sleeve. Deanna laughed and acquiesced.

Meg left Deanna to her tumbling and turned back to the front of the camp. She saw Frank nodding good-bye to a couple of the older boys and hurried to catch up to him.

"Hey, Frank, wait up."

Frank looked over at Meg and he stopped to wait for her.

"So tell me about the loyalty oath thing."

Frank sighed and resumed walking. Meg fell into place next to him. Meg had to walk quickly to keep up with the pace of his long legs.

"It's a questionnaire designed to determine who is really loyal to America and who isn't."

"OK." That seemed to Meg like the kind of thing that could have been done before putting everyone in a camp. And, of course, the little orphan children in the camp nursery weren't old enough to read a loyalty oath, much less spy for Japan. Yet they were here, too.

"As if they would believe the answers," Frank griped.

"So why do it now?"

"Because they want soldiers."

"They want Japanese-Americans they've put in prison camps to fight for America?"

"Yes."

"Would these soldiers fight in Japan? Against Japan?"

"We will fight wherever they need us."

It wasn't lost on Meg that Frank had used the word "we."

"So you would enlist?"

"Of course I will."

"Why?"

Frank stopped and looked at Meg. "It's the right thing to do. Our country is at war. And we need to show that we're loyal Americans, ready to fight. Then perhaps we'll be respected."

"That's your choice?"

"For me, it's not a choice. One of the worst parts of being sent here is not being able to enter the war. At least now they're seeing us as worthy to fight for our country."

Meg wasn't sure she should say it, but she did. "Is it really about respect, though, Frank, or is it just about needing more soldiers?"

"Doesn't matter. We'll earn honor when we fight."

Meg's heart dropped. She had no doubt that Frank loved his country, but here in the camp at least he was safe from battle. Meg realized suddenly that his safety mattered a lot to her. But she could see that being deprived of the risk of battle, and the glory of fighting for his country, annoyed Frank. It diminished him. If his country was finally claiming him, he would go.

"So you'll sign the loyalty oath?"

"Yes," Frank said shortly, but then he abruptly sat on the wooden steps of one of the barracks. "But there's a problem."

"What?" Meg sat down beside Frank.

"There's a question about whether we're willing to serve in combat in the Army."

"So?"

"I can answer yes, but they're making everyone say 'yes' or 'no', even the older ones." Frank paused. "My father will answer no."

Meg couldn't think of any delicate way to ask: "Isn't he too old to enlist anyway?"

"Doesn't matter. Same questionnaire."

"So maybe he should just check 'yes.'"

"How can he answer yes? He's too frail to go."

"Let me see it," Meg demanded.

Frank pointed at question 27.

"See?" Meg said. "It just asks about willingness to serve. It doesn't say you'll have to go."

Frank looked at Meg helplessly. "The next question's even worse."

Meg read it out loud. "Will you swear unqualified allegiance to the United States of America and faithfully defend the United States from any or all attack by foreign or domestic forces, and forswear any form of allegiance or obedience to the Japanese emperor, or any other foreign government, power of organization?"

Meg looked up at Frank. "You were born here. You are American."

"My father was, too."

"So you don't have loyalty to Japan."

"The problem is the word 'forswear.'"

Forswear? Meg looked at it again.

"Forswear means give up, like we used to pledge allegiance to Japan and are now giving up. We can't foreswear something we never had."

"So what?"

"It's like admitting something that might be used against us. Admitting we were loyal to Japan at some point."

Meg inspected the question carefully. "But it also says 'any,' Frank, see that? It says 'any form of,' which could suggest there never was any."

"It doesn't say any allegiance. It says any form of allegiance."

"It's just wording."

"It's an oath. It's the wording of our lives. Wording that decides what our country is going to do next with us."

"You can't rewrite it? Edit it to make it clearer?"

"That would look suspicious, don't you think? And Meg, if we're never getting out of camp, some families would rather be traded back to Japan. If they say yes on this questionnaire, and forswear any allegiance, they can never go back. They won't have any country at all."

"This whole thing is so strange," Meg exclaimed. "Moving everyone here, setting up the camps, and then just asking the prisoners after the fact 'oh and by the way, are you loyal after all?' If so, your sons can go fight and the rest of you can just go home."

"Shh, Meg." Frank looked around to see who was listening. He stepped off the bottom step and started walking away. Meg followed, walking right next to him.

"Our families won't get to go home, even if we enlist." Frank shrugged.

Meg didn't understand. "You'd go fight, even with your family imprisoned by the country you're fighting for?"

"Especially because my family's here," Frank said fiercely. "This is how we prove that we're Americans. This is how we prove that putting us here was wrong. Meg, I tried to enlist more than a year ago, right after Pearl Harbor, but they wouldn't take me. Now they want me, so I will go."

Meg imagined what the camp would be like after all the young men were sent off to war. No big boys playing basketball or teaching judo.

The same thing was happening outside the camp, of course. The senior class in the Owens Valley High School had dwindled to just a few girls. Every day the newspaper listed Owens Valley men who were deploying or already fighting. Frank would go, and leave his family behind, like any other young American man.

The problem was, Frank's father, the same one who would give his son away, would say no on the loyalty oath. That meant that while Frank was fighting, his own father could be considered an enemy.

## *The Rocks*

Japanese-Americans enlisted in the fight. It was time for the uranium ore left behind in the Congo to do the same. Just as Manzanar disgorged its young men into the war effort, General Groves wanted the Shinkolobwe mine to disgorge its entire store of uranium into the U.S. war machine.

The rocks had to sneak by the Nazi ships and submarines to get to America. The Americans shoveled the uranium ore into burlap bags stamped "Product of Bolivia." Bolivia didn't have the best uranium in the world. Nothing to see here. Thus disguised, shipments of uranium rocks made it to American shores right in the middle of wartime. Only two cargo loads were lost at sea.

Even the tailings of the Shinkolobwe mine were freakishly rich in uranium. The waste piles of mining leftovers measured up to 20 percent pure uranium, still higher than any other ore in any other mine anywhere else in the world. The Americans took those mine tailings, too.

The rocks made their intercontinental journey across the ocean, then up to the mills of Canada, down to the enrichment plants of Tennessee, and finally over to the scientists in New Mexico. The rocks traveled under nonsense code names like "tuballoy" or "yttrium."

These two supply streams passed each other above the bitter brine of the Atlantic Ocean: American soldiers heading east to test their resolve in battle, and uranium ore heading west to fulfill its own unique destiny.

# Chapter 17
# Enlisted

## *Meg*

The entire Binnenkerk family assembled inside the front gate of Manzanar. Amy was in Father's arms, and she rested her head against his shoulder, quiet for once. Mother was dressed up and buttoned up in her overcoat, even though it was finally getting warmer. Walter and Meg stood together. The first enlistees, young men from Manzanar, were headed off to war. They would remain state-side for basic training and then deploy to Italy and France.

A sizeable contingent of residents from Independence and Lone Pine had showed up for the send-off. Meg was surprised to see Mr. Evans among them. He must have closed the gas station for the occasion.

The towns had supplied each boy with an extra pair of socks. The church gave each one a small copy of the

New Testament. President Roosevelt had announced the formation of the $442^{nd}$ Infantry Regimental Combat Team, with squadrons of Japanese-American fighters, by saying, "Americanism is not, and never was, a matter of race or ancestry."

Was that true, though? Meg thought of the orphan babies, rounded up and moved into Manzanar just because one or both of their parents was Japanese. They lived in the Children's Village in Manzanar, cared for by nurses instead of parents, for no reason other than their Japanese ancestry. Was the President saying that Americanism was not a matter of race or ancestry because he wanted to make that ideal true? Was he saying that to remind Americans what the evidence around Meg showed many of them had forgotten?

The local Paiute Indian chief was there, too, for the Manzanar send-off. Seeing him popped a little fire cracker in Meg's brain. Maybe that's the way America was, Meg thought. Here were descendants of African slaves and the descendants of displaced Indians joining to honor Japanese-American prisoners heading out to fight for them all. Maybe that's the way America was,

Meg thought. America pummeled you and then enlisted you.

Meg thought the enlistees might march in some kind of formation to the gate, like a miniature parade. She was wrong. Each young man walked with his family toward the bus.

Meg saw Deanna, and then, next to her, there was Frank. He was in full uniform, pressed, creased, ready to go. Mr. and Mrs. Matsumoto followed behind. Mrs. Matsumoto was attired in her most regal kimono, a small embroidered scarf in her hands. No doubt she had made the scarf for Frank to take with him.

Mr. Matsumoto was waking more slowly, as if each step caused him pain. Father had told Meg that Mr. Matsumoto had indeed checked no and no on the loyalty questionnaire. What would that mean for the Matsumoto family? Would Frank's enlistment ease the shame of his father joining the "no-no boys"?

Frank stepped away from his family and strode deliberately toward the bus. Meg found herself unable to look at anyone else. His thick black hair, usually unruly, was controlled and contained by his military cap. Likely it would be short-shaved upon arrival at basic training. His brand-new boots were spit-polished to a dark sheen. A modest khaki duffle was swung over one shoulder.

Meg felt her heart thump. A sliding feeling tickled from the back of her head and down to her ankles. It wasn't a particularly pleasant feeling. It felt sort of like slipping on the monkey bars on the school playground, that instant before thumping onto the ground.

She was having a crush on Frank, Meg realized. A crush felt exactly like getting crushed.

Meg had thought herself beneath Frank's notice. Frank was an older brother, a college student, now a soldier. By contrast, Meg was near to invisible, in a good way, Meg thought. Meg appreciated her near-invisibility. It allowed her to slip from school in Independence to church at Manzanar without unwelcome attention.

The thin sun shone relentlessly white and yellow. A sudden swirl of wind stirred and kicked the gravel base of the camp land. The boys from Manzanar would later find a pinch of sand in the folds of their pant cuffs.

Meg watched as Frank leaned out from the top step of the bus to give his family a quick salute. He walked down the center aisle and slung his duffle up onto the rack. He slid into the seat, pulled the window down, and waved.

Meg felt her throat tighten. Frank was leaving just as Meg realized how important he was. Was that her future riding away on that bus?

In a way, Frank was off to fight two wars. One was the war against Germany and Japan, the other a war for pride and reputation. Meg didn't want to exempt Frank from the battle. He should go. He had to go.

Meg sighed. Would Walter go, too, eventually? He was too young to enlist now, but how long would the war drag on? Meg glanced over at Walter. Meg couldn't imagine Walter wanting to be a soldier, but he might not have any choice. He could definitely be a radio operator, or he could design rockets. Or did he hate the whole enterprise? Meg just couldn't tell.

Meg's focus shifted to Deanna, who just looked cross. Was she angry that Frank had chosen to enlist, or jealous that Frank was getting to leave the camp? If the government came back to Manzanar seeking nurses, would Deanna go, too?

Deanna crossed her arms, perhaps because of the wind but more likely because of temper. *Why am I* watching Deanna, Meg wondered, when this might be the last minute in the world that I get to see Frank?

If she and Frank were dating, Meg would run up to the bus and reach up for a last smile or kiss. But they weren't courting. Frank was a soldier, a man. Meg was still a child.

Tears welled up. Meg's eyes stung in the Manzanar dust. Frank smiled at her, directly at her, and then he gave her a little nod, with a tilt of his head. Meg's tears spilled over. Even if she was still a child, Frank did see her.

The engine of the bus started, startling everyone. The enlistees jostled into the seats, many of them turning forward, no longer looking back. The bus pulled forward, passing the crowd of family members and onlookers. The bus honked, but no one waved.

These first prisoners freed from Manzanar weren't going home to California, but off to war. How ironic that these young men who'd had guns pointed at them every day from guard towers in Manzanar would now be issued the same guns to brandish on behalf of the same Army. The crowd breathed and sighed together as the bus pulled through the guard gate and turned right. Then each person in the crowd breathed and sighed separately, no longer united, as the bus spat up a small stream of grit and accelerated down the road.

The families, so smartly dressed, now just looked forlorn. They first lost their freedom, then their sons. Deanna turned and walked away. Meg thought about following her. She decided against it. Today was not the day to try to restore her friendship with Deanna. There was too much grief there. Meg would leave her alone with it.

## *The Rocks*

Even rural Tennessee was too crowded for what General Groves wanted Dr. Fermi to do next. It was one thing to build giant Calutrons along a river in Tennessee, but now Dr. Fermi and Dr. Woods, now married and called Dr. Marshall, were charged with constructing gigantic plutonium factories. What they were about to do would produce the most poisonously radioactive polluted place on the planet.

The U.S. Army Corps of Engineers requisitioned more than half a million acres of land in southeastern Washington State. Just as in Tennessee, the government told the people who lived there that they would receive a small payment for their land and gave them less than a month to ship out. That included Native American families whose tribes had inhabited the land for centuries.

Why this spot in Washington State? Because the mighty Columbia River flowed through it, down from Canada before curving west to the Pacific Ocean. That water could support both critical functions for plutonium manufacturing: hydro-electric power to run the plants themselves and water to cool the irradiated rods of uranium fuel.

Dr. Fermi designed the massive reactors and the DuPont company built them. Dr. Marshall moved on site to supervise this new western town, an enormous ranch not for roping steers and running cattle, but for farming neutrons and feeding them to uranium in graphite piles the size of ocean cliffs.

Once the fuel rods were irradiated, they would be cooled in deep pools of chilled Columbia River water, then lowered into chemical baths to dissolve the spent uranium and harvest the plutonium. The toxic leftovers were packed into million-gallon underground steel and concrete storage tanks; soon, "tank farms" sprouted all over the area. Even water was enlisted in the war effort.

# Chapter 18
# Thirst

*Meg*

Meg stepped out of school and found with surprise that Walter was waiting to walk home with her for once. She wondered if he had something to say, but he just fell into step next to her. Silently they turned down the street and headed for home.

As they headed north toward their tiny house, Meg saw a panel truck stopped up ahead on the other side of the road. It looked familiar. It was the truck from Manzanar, used to haul everything from camp produce to the camouflage netting woven in the camp factory.

Meg looked to see if Deanna had gotten on the work crew. Sure enough, as they approached, they could see the camp's agricultural foreman slide out from under the truck and Deanna bent over the open hood looking into the engine. Deanna kicked the front wheel, then spun around to see Meg and Walter standing by the side of the road.

"Worthless pile of rust," Deanna said, and slammed the hood down.

The camp foreman pushed himself up to standing and brushed the gravel off his hands. He looked over at at Walter and said, "Starter's out. Axel's about gone, too."

Walter just nodded. He handed Meg his schoolbooks.

"Evans' gas station is right up there." Walter nodded up the road. "We'll have to turn the truck the other way."

"OK," the foreman said. "I'll put it in neutral."

The foreman climbed into the cabin, released the brake, and shifted the gears. Walter crossed the road and went to the back of the truck. Deanna joined him and put her hands on the tail gate next to Walter's. Together, they pushed. Fortunately, the truck was empty. The truck rolled slightly forward. Deanna and Walter added more pressure, while the foreman turned the steering wheel. Meg glanced up the road in both directions. Thankfully, no other vehicles were coming. Once the truck had turned to face north, the foreman straightened out the wheel. Working together, Deanna and Walter got the truck rolling at a steady pace. Meg walked alongside.

As they approached the gas station, Mr. Evans emerged from the office, wearing his ubiquitous denim overalls and cap. He stepped toward the pumps and waited for the truck. There was a little rut between the roadside and gas station. The truck fell into the slight dip but Walter and Deanna kept pushing. The front wheels lifted out of the dip and the truck continued forward.

"See if you can steer it over there." Mr. Evans pointed toward the open bay in his garage. Meg wasn't sure they could navigate between the pumps and the stack of old tires, but they did. The foreman braked gently, then set the parking brake and lowered himself out of the truck.

He reached out to shake hands with Mr. Evans. "Tanaka," he introduced himself. "I run agricultural programs for the camp."

"Will Evans."

"And this is my farm apprentice," Mr. Tanaka said, gesturing toward Deanna.

Farm apprentice, thought Meg. How had Deanna managed to swing that?

They stood, looking at the non-functioning truck.

"If you don't mind us leaving it here, I can get a crew over tomorrow to look at it," Mr. Tanaka said.

"If it's just the battery or starter, I could fix it myself," Mr. Evans said. "Otherwise, you'll need a mechanic."

"It's the Army's truck," Mr. Tanaka said. "They'll have to take care of it. We can just walk back to camp from here."

"It's seven miles or more," Mr. Evans said. "I'd drive you, but my nephew took the wrecker up to Bishop. You can use the telephone in the office, though."

"I'll see if the Director can come and get us," Mr. Tanaka decided. They might not be welcome to walk through town and it wasn't likely a passing car would pick up hitchhikers with Japanese faces.

While he made the call, Meg waved at Deanna.

"Hi," Meg called.

Deanna spun and walked away.

Embarrassed, Meg turned away. Through the large glass window of the service station, Meg could see Mr.

Tanaka talking on the wall-mounted phone. Mr. Evans had settled down into his office chair. The chair reclined so far backward Meg thought it a wonder that Mr. Evans didn't tip over onto his head. Probably he sat there just like that every day.

She ought to grab Walter and head home, Meg thought.

Meg saw Walter step out from the gas station hallway, wiping his hands on a rag. He settled down in the metal folding chair next to Mr. Evans' desk. It didn't look like he'd be heading home for a while.

Meg would have liked to keep Deanna company while she waited for a ride, but Deanna was snubbing her.

Feeling uncertain, Meg walked toward the gas station office and stepped inside. There weren't any other chairs. Under the broad window was a wide sill with a very dusty plant and some yellowed catalogs for engine parts. Meg slid them to one side and perched on the windowsill, keeping their schoolbooks on her lap.

Mr. Tanaka hung up. "They'll come get us. Thanks for use of the phone."

"No problem," Mr. Evans said companionably.

"I hope we get that truck back in order. We're due to pick up a load of irrigation pipes tomorrow."

"What'll that be for?" Walter asked.

"We're getting livestock," Mr. Tanaka said. "Cows. Hay barn's going up and we're adding some watering troughs."

"You used to be a cowboy, didn't you?' Walter asked Mr. Evans.

"My grandfather was," he answered. "He came out here as a Buffalo Soldier."

"What's that?" Meg asked, forgetting the discomfort of sitting on a dusty windowsill.

"After slave times, the Army wouldn't take the Coloreds but there was a cavalry attachment of Negro soldiers stationed on the other side of the mountains."

"No kidding," Walter said. "What did they do?"

"Fought the Indians, among other things. Fought forest fires. Built roads. My grandpa was honorably discharged, and he bought some heads of cattle."

"Why were they called Buffalo Soldiers?" Meg wondered. "Were there buffalos?"

"No, not around here. The name came from the first time the Indians saw colored folk. That's the name that stuck. Well, one of the names, anyway."

"Does your family still have cattle here?" Walter asked.

"Nope," Mr. Evans said.

"Why not?"

"Water," Mr. Evans said shortly.

"What do you mean?" Meg asked.

"Government took the water rights, oh fifteen, twenty years ago," Mr. Evans said.

"Just took it?" Walter asked.

"Well, they bought the land and the water rights that went with it. Now all our water goes down the Los Angeles aqueduct."

"That's why the camp's here, then," Meg guessed. "Because the government owns the land?"

"Yup, that's all government land. Interesting idea to put cows back. I guess they'll let you use water since they're government cows."

Meg pictured the beautiful rushing streams cutting through the camp. She had never thought of them as government-owned streams. Apparently the water wasn't as free as it looked.

"Is that why the orchards between here and the camp are dead?" Meg asked suddenly.

"Yep. You know Manzanar means apple orchard in Spanish," Mr. Evans said. "Kind of a joke, naming the camp after a dried up orchard."

If the families had thought they were being moved into an apple orchard, they sure were set up for disappointment.

Meg thought about Mr. Fujii's chrysanthemum greenhouse, Peace Park, and the tiny piped-in ponds between some of the barracks. How strange that just because the government forced people into this dried-up place, now some of the water could stay a while. What would happen when the camp closed? Those little bits of garden would all dry up. The water would be turned off again, like a giant spigot.

What a sad conversation, Meg thought, looking out the window and watching Deanna standing by the side of the road.

Meg couldn't imagine a more improbable grouping of people than at that little service station in the middle of California: the Negro grandson of a Buffalo Soldier, two Japanese-Americans who were supposedly enemy aliens, and two white Americans who had lived most of their lives in Japan.

Meg wasn't one to think there was any reason for the paths of those five people to cross at that moment. It wasn't destiny. It was just war and history. It was just the strange and ordinary complexity of life. People moved or were drawn or pushed from place to place, maybe by choice, maybe by chance, but mostly because of forces outside their control, circumstances to be survived if possible. The moves were just things to make the best of, that was all. The only thing to do was appreciate the beauty in the randomness. The only thing to do was to drink the water while it flowed.

Just then, not one but two vehicles pulled into the station and the incongruities doubled. First was Director Merritt's large black sedan. Out he came, wearing his suit jacket over a sweater vest. Second was an ancient pick-up truck with a Paiute Indian family crammed inside. There were at least four adults sitting in the front and at least three children in the back.

Meg felt a smile bubble up from her heart. Meg had only lived in places where almost all the people looked the same, first in Tsu, Japan where her family were the only white people, and more recently in Michigan, where everyone was white. Now the people around her were as mixed up as gumballs in a jar.

Mr. Tanaka walked out to greet Director Merritt and take him over to inspect the ailing truck. Mr. Evans pitched forward, launching his long frame out of his desk chair to go serve his customer. Walter followed him out, picking up a rag and bucket to clean their windows.

Alone in the service station office, Meg just watched. There was Deanna, kicking rocks, the Indian family sitting silently in the cab of their truck, Director Merritt in his dress shoes, and Mr. Evans and Mr. Tanaka in their work coveralls. If there's any place I belong, Meg thought, this is it.

Impulsively, Meg walked outside and over to Director Merritt. "Hi. Can I ride with you back to the camp? I'll get a ride home with my father."

Director Merritt nodded. Meg ran back to the service station to gather the schoolbooks for Walter to take home. Then she climbed into the big black sedan and waited for Deanna. The time had come to make Deanna talk to her, and forgive her. Mr. Tanaka climbed into the front seat. Now Deanna had no place to sit other than next to Meg.

## *The Rocks*

Secrecy was wearing on the friendship between the U.S. and England. England had extremely gifted scientists like Dr. Chadwick, the first to identify neutrons. Dr. Meitner's nephew Dr. Frisch had resettled in England, as had Dr. Rotblat from Poland. England didn't have the Shinkolobwe rocks, and they certainly didn't have giant factories to enrich U235 or manufacture plutonium, but they were advancing in nuclear research in other ways.

Was secrecy slowing the U.S. down? Could bringing the British scientists into the fold speed things up? In August of 1943, President Roosevelt and Britain's Prime Minister Winston Churchill met secretly in Quebec, Canada and came to an agreement. The Yankees and the Brits would share freely all they had learned about how to make an atomic bomb.

And they would promise for eternity to never use the bomb against each other.

# Chapter 19
# Allies

*Meg*

Father had brought a guest home for dinner. He was about as tall as Father but his build was considerably different. Where Father was slight and straight, this man was stocky and muscular. Where Father had a mustache, this man had a full beard. Where Father was slow to smile, this man laughed like a bear, with full-throated chuckles and guffaws coursing up from his chest.

"Mr. Adams is a photographer," Father said. Mr. Adams had parked his big cargo car in their driveway. Inside were large mysterious objects covered with blankets: his photography equipment.

Mr. Adams told them stories about driving high up into the Sierra Nevadas, waiting for nightfall, and leaving his car behind and hiking up towards the crest, carrying his camera equipment.

"Are you heading into the mountains tomorrow?" Walter asked.

"No," Father answered for Mr. Adams. "He is going into the camp for the next few days."

"Into Manzanar?" Meg was surprised. Photographs weren't allowed in the prison camp.

"I'm on a special assignment from the government," Mr. Adams said, "to show what life is like in the camp."

"I thought you only took pictures of mountains and trees," Meg said.

"Oh, I guess I can take pictures of people too." Mr. Adams smiled.

Mr. Adams stayed a couple of days, taking pictures in the camp, and then he and Father went hiking up into the Sierras. Meg noticed that when Father was with Mr. Adams, Father laughed. Father seemed stronger. Meg hoped Mr. Adams would come back soon. He promised the next time he came through, he would take Meg and Walter hiking, too.

Meg wasn't sure that would really happen, but, sure enough, Mr. Adams came back for a second visit to Manzanar, he and Father made good on their promise to take Meg and Walter up into the mountains. Even Mother said yes. So here they were, bouncing up a dirt road, switch-backing into the high Sierras, catching glimpses of snow patches in the clefts above.

That wasn't even the most extraordinary part. The most amazing thing was that Deanna was sitting next to her in Mr. Adams' truck. Father had put in for a day release permit for Deanna. Day release was supposed to be for work only, but Director Merritt gave special permission.

Deanna was still technically a prisoner, but for this one day, Meg and Deanna were climbing so high into the Sierra mountains that Manzanar - its rows of splintery shacks and wooden guard towers - could scarcely be seen below.

It was almost as though the camp wasn't even there. The mountains rose up around them, permanent, eternal. Manzanar down at the base of dusty Owens Valley could just blow away, draped in mounds of sand, leaving only small stacks of rocks.

Meg's only immediate worry was of Mr. Adams' vehicle sliding off the face of the mountain. The car was a cross between a station wagon and a work truck, with an oversized engine that smelled of burnt oil. Mr. Adams drove it like a tank. He slowed only to shift gears and then spurred the car forward, bouncing across ruts made by melting ice.

Walter was sitting on the side that looked out over thin air. Meg was right next to the cliffside, with Deanna squeezed between them. Meg was so close to the wall of rock and dirt that she could have reached out the window to pick a flower.

"The higher we get, the higher we can hike," Mr. Adams said cheerily, turning his head toward the back seat so they could hear him over the roar of the engine.

Every time they reached what looked like a dead-end, what looked like a point of no return, Mr. Adams would make a sharp turn and a trail would materialize. What had once surely been only a deer path had since been widened by lumberjacks and woodsmen. The tires of Mr. Adams' car found familiar ruts to follow.

When they finally came to a stop and Mr. Adams turned his key to cut the engine, the car filled with sudden silence. The people tumbled out, careful not to slip on the wet ground.

"It's so cold!" Walter exclaimed.

Now that they were up and out of Owens Valley, the temperature had plummeted and the wind was blowing.

Deanna shook out her hair, like a dog released from a kennel, and grinned over at Meg.

Meg felt like stretching her arms high above her head, so she did. She lifted her chest and let the cold air fill her inside. Up here, they could leave the worries of war and the camp behind them.

That's what made today so truly exhilarating, Meg realized. Deanna had been so unreachably angry. Even though Wormley was gone, he sure had left poison in his wake. But Deanna had agreed to come on this hike and, already, she was smiling.

They set off on the trail, Mr. Adams setting the pace. Walter pressed forward, wanting to walk with the men. Meg could hear the rumbling of Mr. Adams' story-telling even though she couldn't hear the words.

Mr. Adams wasn't carrying a camera today, but his hands weren't idle for long. He gestured, and pointed, and touched, and framed pictures with his hands. Walter followed and listened, keeping up with every footstep. For once, Meg's father didn't have to be on call. Father nodded when Mr. Adams gestured out to the mountains and said, "This is my church."

Things can get better, Meg realized. Then she wondered why that thought had crossed her mind. Had things become bad?

Deanna was doing better than keeping up. The more they hiked, the nimbler Deanna became, climbing over large rocks instead of stepping around them. The pace was a bit brisk from Meg's point of view, but she was determined not to be the one to ask for a rest.

They reached a large outcropping of rock. Mr. Adams stepped confidently out to the edge. Meg inched closer and looked down. Just a ribbon of the road could be seen in the valley, and a row of buildings that must have be the town of Independence. Further up the mountain along the left, Meg could see Mr. Adam's car, engine off, waiting patiently to carry them back down.

Mr. Adams was talking about the geography and geology of the mountain range. Meg was occupied with breathing and looking.

"Aren't there mountain lions up here?" Walter asked.

"Oh, all the mountain lions know me," Mr. Adams answered. "Nothing to worry about there."

"Do you feed them?" asked Meg.

"That's the worst thing I could do." Mr. Adams shook his head. "I can't have mountain lions thinking I'm here to take care of them. I'm not bringing them food and I don't want to be their food."

"Have you ever gotten a picture of a mountain lion?" Walter wanted to know.

"Not yet," Mr. Adams admitted. "It's easier to take pictures of things that don't move quite so fast."

"But there was one time," he continued, then paused for effect. "One time, I dropped a Hershey bar on the ground. I was setting up my camera and frankly, I just plain forgot about it. And with that brown wrapper, well, as the day ended, it just blended in on the ground. By the time I thought to look for it, I couldn't find it."

"That night, as I lay on my bedroll trying to fall asleep, thinking about apertures, and angles, and whether the morning fog would ruin my shot, I heard a snuffling sound, then paper ripping."

"Your chocolate bar," Meg breathed.

"Yup. That was the end of my Hershey bar."

"A mountain lion," said Walter.

"I can't be sure," Mr. Adams admitted. "Whoever it was wanted the chocolate bar more than I did, so that was the end of that."

"It could've been a bear," Father said.

"Could've been," Mr. Adams agreed. "Better a chocolate bar goes missing than me."

Pressing higher into the mountains, they came to a rockfall that completely blocked the trail. Mr. Adams climbed up onto the rocks. "We're close, now. Right on the other side is a glacial lake."

As they stepped carefully from rock to rock, Meg noticed a thin rivulet of water flowing in a channel between the rock. The rivulet joined into a stream, dancing downward. That's where the water came from for Manzanar, and for the apple trees that used to grow in Owens Valley.

The glacial lake was smaller than Meg had imagined, just a circular pond, icy to the touch and so reflective that every cloud in the sky was mirrored on its surface.

Father passed around a Thermos of lemonade. When it was empty, he refilled it with the sweet mountain water. Meg's mother had packed thick sandwiches for them, wrapped in wax paper. The sandwiches were ham salad with spicy pickles. Even Mr. Adams ate one with appreciation.

The silence was fierce. Deanna took one bite of sandwich, set it aside and lay back on the cold rock, as if she needed silence more than food. A solo hawk floated lazily above them, inspecting. The air felt so thin that Meg couldn't even hear her own breathing.

A brown furry creature waddled around a rock, then stepped in the little clearing by the glacial lake. It was much larger than a squirrel. It looked to Meg like a beaver, except without a flapping tail. Meg held perfectly still, hoping it would come closer.

The animal paused to sniff at a patch of moss, then nibbled at a clump of light purple columbine springing up from a crevice in the rock.

The creature didn't seem to read their presence at all. Perhaps since humans weren't expected, they were ignored, or simply unacknowledged.

"Hey, Deanna," Meg called out softly. "Look over there."

The animal lifted its head, angled its nose, and ambled along out of sight. Meg felt her heart unfold like an origami crane, like a yellow chrysanthemum opening its petals to the sun. She caught Deanna's eye. Deanna looked back at Meg, alert and watchful.

"What was that? A muskrat? A badger?" Walter guessed.

"A marmot," Mr. Adams said. "A yellow-bellied marmot, to be precise."

"A scaredy-cat, huh?" Walter joked. "That's why he's yellow-bellied?"

"No," Mr. Adams said mildly. "It's just about the color of fur on his belly. Although if you want to give him a nickname, some people call them 'whistle pigs.'"

Sure enough, they could hear a thin whistle coming from the other side of the rock. No doubt the marmot was warning others about the intruders on their mountain.

"You gotta call things by their name," Mr. Adams said. "That's how you know you're getting it right."

## *The Rocks*

The British landed in Los Alamos. Dr. Chadwick and Dr. Frisch got right to work. For Dr. Rotblat, there was a hiccup. He had accepted England's offer of safe haven, but he never became a British citizen. He was

Polish through and through and determined to return to Poland as soon as the war ended. But the Quebec agreement was only between the U.S. and England. The deal didn't include Poland or Polish citizens. Eventually, General Groves made an exception and allowed Dr. Rotblat to start work in Los Alamos.

It was helpful to have fresh eyes. The British scientists were amazed at the problems the Americans had already solved in the quest for a bomb. They were all keenly aware of the Nazi threat and knew the Germans hadn't stopped trying to build a bomb, too.

Having rejected graphite as a moderator, the Germans were experimenting with deuterium water as a way to control the flow of neutrons over to the uranium. The Nazis seized a hydroelectric power plant in Norway that produced deuterium water. Knowing what the water could be used for, the Allies bombed the power plant. In February of 1944, the Germans tried moving the undamaged barrels of deuterium water across Lake Tinn for transport into Germany. Norwegian commandos got word of the plan and sank the ferry. That brought an end to another ingredient Germany could have used in a nuclear recipe.

This tremendous news from Norway didn't lessen the pressure or pace for General Groves one whit. To him, the development of the bomb wasn't just about halting Nazi advances across Europe. He was looking farther into the future. For him, the development of the bomb was about positioning the U.S. as a world superpower. Germany was the most immediate concern, but not the only threat on the horizon. In March of 1944, General Groves remarked to Dr. Rotblat that Russia would likely become the more dangerous foe in years to come.

The comment shocked Dr. Rotblat. Over in Poland, it was the Russians who were risking life and limb to push the Germans back. Russia was an ally, but not only that, Russia was Poland's best hope for evicting the Nazis.

What General Groves regarded as loyalty to his country was perceived by Dr. Rotblat as disloyalty to his. It dawned on Dr. Rotblat that while the Los Alamos scientists remained focused on defeating Germany, to General Groves, the terms of their mission had already changed. To General Groves, the goal was no longer just victory over Germany. The goal was the bomb itself and the world dominance it would represent, in particular, to intimidate Russia.

# Chapter 20
# Changing the Terms

*Meg*

Meg entered Manzanar camp for church and was surprised to see Deanna in the congregation with her family. Meg broke away from her family and sat next to Deanna. Whether Deanna made it through the whole service or not, Meg wanted to sit by her side.

Deanna stayed. Soon it was time to sing the Doxology. "Praise God from whom all blessings flow." Then Deanna began to tinker with the words. "Praise Her all creatures here below. Praise Her above, ye heavenly host. Praise Mother, Daughter, Holy Ghost. Amen."

Deanna smiled.

Sitting on her metal folding chair, Meg stared at Walter's back. Walter seemed to be sitting a little straighter, a little more attentively. He had heard

Deanna change the words, making God and Jesus female.

Deanna tilted her head slightly and whispered to Meg, "You gotta call things by their name. That's how you know you're getting it right."

Meg liked it. Meg smiled. Deanna was healing.

After church, Meg didn't want to be parted from Deanna.

"Do you want to see the cows?" Deanna asked.

"Sure."

The girls walked toward the agricultural barn. There was Mr. Tanaka, driving a pick-up truck loaded with alfalfa to the center of the dry pasture. The cows came sauntering over, recognizing the truck that brought them food. They were calves, mostly, black and brown.

Mr. Tanaka and Deanna swung up in the back of the truck and started lifting the heavy bales to throw over the side. Mr. Tanaka handed Meg a metal rake to spread the alfalfa out. Cows pushed around her, large and warm, nuzzling into the feed.

"Making friends?" Deanna asked, dryly, looking down at Meg.

"Yes," Meg answered.

The pitch fork was longer and heavier than Meg anticipated. The nearest cow eyed her. Meg stopped for a moment and looked back at the cow. The cow had a sweet black outline around its eyes, and a velvety lashes. Then the cow mooed and the spell was broken.

"Alright, let's stack the rest of these bales in the barn," Mr. Tanaka said.

Meg climbed up into the back of the truck and sat with Deanna among the remaining bales for a bouncing hayride to Manzanar's new barn.

Across the highway, a swarm of little black birds lifted up from the field and circled together, first left, then right, then settled back down again on a different part of the field. Meg wondered if there was enough food left there for them to pick.

By the front gate, Meg could see a slick black military vehicle pull into the camp. Two officers emerged from the car and Director Merritt came out to greet them. Then Meg and Deanna saw tiny Mrs. Ito standing next to Director Merritt. The guests handed her a folded American flag.

Meg grabbed Deanna's arm. "What happened?"

"It's got to be Taro."

That was Mrs. Ito's son.

"Oh, no," Meg said. A folded flag could only mean one thing: a Manzanar boy killed in action.

"Now they'll put a gold star on her barracks," Deanna said.

"She'll still be here, a prisoner in camp," Meg said.

"But she'll have a gold star instead of a son."

Mr. Tanaka stopped the truck so they could slide off and head over to see what comfort they could offer.

## *The Rocks*

Town by town, country by country, the Allies reclaimed German-occupied territory, marching triumphantly into liberated Paris in August of 1944. General Groves dispatched science spies to travel with the Allied troops. Their first goal was to sleuth out how far the Germans had actually gotten in their bomb program. Their second goal was to scoop up all bomb-making materials, schematics, and scientists before Russia could get them. General Groves was prepared to honor the Quebec accord, but no further. For the U.S. and England to hold a global monopoly on nuclear technology, they had to capture Germany's remaining scientists before Russia could get them.

Most of the German scientists had cycled through the Paris laboratory of Dr. Irène Joliot-Curie during the four years of Nazi occupation, so she and her husband Dr. Frédéric Joliot-Curie were in a good position to know how far the Germans had gotten in their efforts toward a bomb. Dr. Frédéric Joliot-Curie assured the science spies that the Germans had made very little progress toward a bomb. They hadn't figured out how to separate U235 from U238, Dr. Joliot-Curie said. They hadn't gotten a chain reaction to work. The news was reassuring, but General Groves wasn't about to take one scientist's word for it.

Just weeks later, General Groves' science spies were able to get into Belgium. Belgian nationals helped the spies track the location where the Nazis had buried the Shinkolobwe ore. The Americans dug it up and sent it packing off to Canada for processing and then down to Tennessee for enrichment. The Shinkolobwe ore left behind in Belgium would now join the war machine on the American side.

So far, their mission was a complete success, but until the science spies could get into Germany and capture Dr. Hahn and Dr. Heisenberg, General Groves couldn't be completely sure what Dr. Joliot-Curie had said was true: the Germans had nothing.

While the science spies were busy in Europe, Dr. Fermi and Dr. Marshall loaded the first slugs of U238 into the fully operational reactors in Washington. The war in Europe was drawing to a slow and violent end, but plutonium production on a massive scale was just getting started. The Americans were still a year or more away from a plutonium bomb.

Dr. Fermi had achieved all he set out to do, but his dream had never been to build an atomic bomb. What drove Dr. Fermi was a hunger for knowledge to understand the properties and potentials of all the exquisite minerals and elements in Nature. Dr. Fermi's dream was science, not warfare.

General Groves served a different master. His assignment was to hand the American president atomic capability and to do it before, and to the exclusion of, anyone else. By the summer of 1944, General Groves knew full well the bomb effort wouldn't end with victory in Europe, or victory in Japan, for that matter. He was executing an enormous tap dance of companies, scientists, spies, airplanes, ships, and trains with the singular goal of making America an atomic super-power for all the generations to come.

General Groves and Dr. Fermi's efforts paralleled for a time, but which of them was thinking about the future? Both of them, really. General Groves was thinking about the political future; Dr. Fermi was thinking about the scientific future.

Dr. Fermi wrote an assessment for other scientists to sign and sent it to the head of the Metallurgical Society which had helped support his very first pile in Chicago. In the letter, he guessed that the Germans were "about as far along as ourselves" in developing a nuclear weapon - Dr. Fermi wasn't privy to the latest intelligence from the science spies. On the false assumption that Germany was about as far along as the Americans, Dr. Fermi resolved that their work in the development of a nuclear bomb couldn't stop. They had to keep going.

But what then? It is my "ardent hope," Dr. Fermi wrote, "that nuclear explosives will never be used to annihilate cities or whole nations." Instead, he wanted the world to pursue nuclear fission for the purposes of generating energy to run whole cities and developing specialized isotopes that could be used to wipe out tumors and cure disease.

Do you remember that conversation that Mr. Sengier had with Colonel Nichols where they mapped out the acquisition of all the Congolese uranium? Do you remember how a single conversation between two people could steer the future of the planet across continents and time? Dr. Fermi intended for his letter to open the next and new conversation about the future of the planet across continents and time.

Unfortunately, General Groves and Dr. Fermi were not having this conversation with each other. The scientists - Dr. Szilárd and Dr. Oppenheimer and Dr. Fermi - wanted a voice in how their scientific discoveries would be used, but they didn't have a seat at the table. They had given their work freely and ultimately, they weren't the owners of what they had made.

When it came right down to it, what Dr. Fermi had was a wish, and what General Groves had was a plan.

# Chapter 21
# They Have Nothing

*Meg*

=Every weekday afternoon, the same ratty, dusty bus came to Manzanar to take a few more Japanese-American families down to the train station in Barstow. From there they could travel east to farms and factories that had agreed to sponsor them with jobs and places to stay. It wasn't an apology. It wasn't "here's your house and your business back." The war was far from over, but the panic that had led to the mass incarceration of Japanese-Americans had ebbed. The families weren't a threat and they were being released, neither indicted nor exonerated. So long as they filled out the loyalty questionnaire the right way. So long as they found a host that would vouch for them. So long as they left and no longer burdened the American government.

Deanna's mother got an offer from a sewing factory in New England. Deanna could finish high school in the mornings and work there in the afternoons. They wouldn't be paid much, but there was a dorm for workers where they could live.

Mr. Matsumoto wasn't going with them. Since he'd answered "no no" on the loyalty questionnaire, he had been moved from Manzanar camp to another camp, and then another, and letters Mrs. Matsumoto had written him came back undelivered. Deanna and her mother no longer knew where he was.

Deanna had gotten a few letters from Frank. He and the $442^{nd}$ Infantry Battalion were in Italy. Piecing together the skimpy information he was allowed to share with what was being broadcast in the newsreels, Deanna discerned that the Allies had broken the Gustav Line and pushed the Germans out of Italy. Japanese-American fighters were distinguishing themselves as some of the most valiant American fighters in the war.

The news from Frank was positive, but Deanna wasn't happy about moving to New Hampshire. "It's cold there," Deanna complained to Meg.

"But Harvard is close by in Massachusetts," Meg said.

"So what?" Deanna was contemptuous. "Harvard doesn't accept women."

Meg smiled. "Radcliffe, then. That's where Helen Keller went to college."

"I'll start saving my pennies," Deanna said dryly.

"Or you could go to Barnard. I could meet you in New York City."

"You're going to meet me for college?"

"Yes!"

"Well, my standards aren't high," Deanna declared. "Any school with ivy on the walls will do."

"We'll meet at a college with ivy on the walls," Meg decided. "You'll finish high school before me, but I'll get there as soon as I can."

"You really think we'll still know each other?"

"Of course I do," Meg said. "I think we're lifelong friends."

"You'll probably still be my only friend," Deanna griped. "Everyone in America hates us."

"Not everyone will hate you just because you're Japanese."

"They'll find other reasons."

"I think things are better on the East Coast," Meg said. "I think there's less prejudice there." Meg wasn't at all sure about that. She remembered being taunted as a "Jap" in Michigan, and she didn't even look Japanese.

"They just want us to work," Deanna continued. "We're just cheap labor to them."

"The factory will probably have other relocated Japanese-Americans."

"That's even worse. If I only wanted to be with Japanese-Americans, I'd stay here."

"What do you want then? Do you want Negro friends? Indian friends? Chinese friends?"

"Yes."

"You want to live in a rainbow."

"I can't feel safe when everyone looks alike. That leads to social rot. There's too much temptation to elevate some people over others for meaningless reasons."

"You want an American quilt, that's what you want," Meg said.

"And I'm not sure I'm ready for a real high school."

"Deanna. You're the smartest person I know."

"I'm pretty sure I'm way behind."

"You'll catch up."

"I'll end up in jail. Someone will say something rude to me, and I won't take it."

Meg felt helpless. "Deanna. You're going to have to figure out what the game is, and win at it. What is it that you want more than anything?"

"Name some more colleges."

Meg thought for a moment. "Oberlin. Cornell. Wesleyan."

Deanna frowned. "More."

"Smith. Vassar. Bryn Mawr. Bryn Mawr, Deanna! We could meet there."

"Why Bryn Mawr?"

"Quaker school. Definitely has ivy. Girls only."

"Okay, Meg Binnenkerk. We will meet again at Bryn Mawr."

"It's a deal. One thing, though."

"What?"

"They don't have cows there. At least I don't think so."

"That's okay. I'll bring my own."

Meg pictured Deanna showing up to college holding a rope connected to the nose ring of a cow.

"Well, that solves that."

"What will it take to get there, Meg?"

"Good grades," Meg said.

"Money," Deanna said.

"Basically, Deanna, just don't get a criminal record."

"You keep coming back to that. Why is that?" Deanna asked with a smile.

"It seems kind of fundamental." Meg looked around at the dusty, empty shacks. "The one who's stuck here now is me."

"You won't be here for long."

"This is why it's really important for you to write to me as soon as you know your address. Promise?"

"Promise," Deanna said.

"I'll bring you an envelope with the address to our house in Independence. All you have to do is fill in your address in New Hampshire or Massachusetts or wherever as soon as you know it."

At the tiny post office in Independence, Meg managed to buy an envelope and stamp and carefully wrote out her address. Inside, Meg tucked a couple of the purple columbine flowers she had pressed in one of Father's Bibles.

When the day for Deanna's departure arrived, Meg raced home from school. Father had promised to take an afternoon break to come home and take Meg back to camp with him.

But Father wasn't there.

There was no car in front and no one home; no one was inside, not even Mother or Amy. Mother wouldn't have been any help anyway, because she didn't know how to drive.

Walter would have to help her.

Meg dumped her schoolbag and grabbed the envelope. She raced around to the shed in back.

"Walter! I need you to help me."

"Help you what?" Walter was putting away his bike.

"Help me get to Manzanar. Right now."

"Is the car here?" Walter looked interested at the prospect of getting behind the wheel.

"No. You have to take me on your bike."

"Meg. It's miles from here."

"I have to get there. Deanna's leaving today with her mother. I promised her I would say good-bye."

"If the car was here, I would drive you."

"Ugh!" Meg yelled. Walter couldn't solve her problem. He didn't really care whether she made it or not. He just wanted to drive the car.

"The gas station," Meg said out loud.

"What are you going to do?"

"I'm going to ask Mr. Evans for help. Let me have your bike."

"No," Walter said, but it was too late. Meg had already mounted the bicycle and started peddling.

"Hey!" Walter yelled. "Be careful!"

"Be careful," muttered Meg. "You were willing to get in Father's car and drive down the highway but you have a complaint about me riding a bike?"

Two quick turns and Meg reached the gas station. She dumped the bike by the open door and flew into the office.

"Mr. Evans!"

"What, child?" Mr. Evans said, coming out from the back wiping his hands on a rag that was already so dirty Meg couldn't see how it could be of any use.

"I need a ride to Manzanar. I need to go right now."

Mr. Evans looked at Meg as if he was befuddled.

Meg took a breath. "Would you please give me a ride to Manzanar? You could close the station. Just for a little while."

"Please?" Meg tried again.

"Well, alright. I can do that for you."

"Thank you, Mr. Evans." Relief flooded through Meg, replaced almost immediately with impatience. Mr. Evans finished, deliberately, wiping his hands. Then he reached slowly over the pegboard and selected a key. Meg knew she should be grateful he didn't have to change his shoes or change out of his oily coveralls.

"Thank you so much," Meg said, instead of what she really wanted to say, which was "hurry up!"

Soon Mr. Evans was behind the wheel of his tow truck. Meg climbed high up into the cab next to him. He pulled forward and stopped to look right and left before pulling out onto the road. His turn signal made a loud "tick, tick, tick." There was nobody coming in either direction.

Eventually he pulled out and to the left and they were rumbling down the road. Meg realized that her right foot was pressing down against the floor board as if she could make the truck go faster. Meg had to tell her foot to be patient, too. They lumbered past the orchard of dead trees and then the Manzanar fence could be seen dotted with guard towers. Meg strained to see the bus at the entrance.

"Please still be there," Meg muttered to herself.

The gate came into view. No bus.

Maybe it hadn't arrived yet.

As Mr. Evans pulled the wrecker over to the side of the road by the camp entrance, Meg slid down out of the cab and landed on the ground.

"Thank you, Mr. Evans!" she called back to him, slamming the heavy tow truck door.

"Do you need me to wait for you, Meg?" Mr. Evans called through the open window.

"No, thank you. I'm sure my father can take me home," Meg called to him, walking backwards toward the gate. Meg paused briefly to make sure the guard in the sentry box saw her. She pointed through the pedestrian gate and he nodded. As soon as she was inside, Meg dashed toward the administration building.

"Miss Moroni! When's the bus coming?"

Miss Moroni looked up, her bent nose poking above the stack of papers on the giant desk.

"Bus?" she asked, scrunching up her face. "Are you sure there's a bus today?"

"Yes," Meg said impatiently. "There's going to be bus today. Deanna's leaving with her mother."

"Oh, I'm not sure that's right," Miss Moroni said, picking up one piece of paper from the stack and placing it down, then another, then another. "Actually," she said, as if reconsidering, "I believe there was a bus for today."

"That's what I thought." Meg frowned.

"That would be the same bus that took Pastor Dale down to the train station, now wouldn't it?" Miss Moroni said with a thoughtful look.

Pastor Dale? Did she mean Wormley? Why on Earth was Miss Moroni talking about him?

"You mean Wormley?" Meg hesitated. "I would imagine it was the same bus."

"That's Pastor Wormley to you, young lady."

"But that was months ago." Meg was confused by the turn in the conversation. Wormley was long gone and good riddance to him.

"Some of us are not so quick to forget," Miss Moroni said crisply. "Such a nice man, called away too soon."

Not at all a nice man, Meg thought. Not at all too soon. What was this about?

"You miss him?" Meg guessed.

"Oh, no, I'm sure it's all the same to me," Miss Moroni said, but that sounded like a lie.

How dense was poor Miss Moroni? Had she thought she was having some kind of romance with

Wormley? The same oh-so-married Wormley who was feeling up Deanna? What was she thinking?

"I'm not here to talk about him," Meg declared. In fact, there was literally nothing she wanted to do less than to talk about Wormley. "I'm trying to find Deanna."

"Well, that's a problem, isn't it, dear?" Miss Moroni said, with a stamp of the stapler into pieces of paper that likely didn't even need to be stapled. "The bus for today is gone, just like every day." Miss Moroni banged on the top of the stapler so hard that the papers on her desk jumped.

"Never mind." Meg spun and dashed out of the administration building, running smack into Director Merritt. "Oh, I'm so sorry!"

"What's going on, Meg?"

"I was trying to catch the bus. To say good-bye to Deanna."

"The bus just left, Meg, only just a few minutes ago."

"Was Deanna on it? I thought she was leaving today. Maybe I was wrong. Maybe it wasn't today."

"Yes, she was on the bus, with her mother. I'm sure she would have liked to say good-bye to you."

"I could've gotten here in time. Father was supposed to come get me."

"I'm sorry, Meg. There was a church meeting that went long. In fact, I don't think the meeting's over yet."

Director Merritt was such a kind man. Meg looked up at him. If Meg couldn't get the envelope to Deanna, Deanna wouldn't have Meg's address. They wouldn't have any way to reach each other. Their friendship would slip away. They would be lost to each other.

Just then, the phone on Miss Moroni's desk jangled.

"Yes, one moment please. He's here," she said to the caller and held out the receiver on the heavy black phone to  Director Merritt.

"Hello?" Meg heard Director Merritt say. "I'm sorry to hear that. Yes, I can bring a fan belt. Did it damage anything when it snapped? No? That's good, anyway."

He hung up and spoke to Miss Moroni. "The bus broke down south of Lone Pine. I'll just head down there to see what we can do."

Meg's hopes lifted. "Please, please may I go with you?"

Director Merritt looked over at Meg. "What would your father say if I took you without asking him first?"

"He would probably say he was sorry he was detained and unable to get me here himself like he promised." Now Meg was lying outrageously. It was wholly unlikely Father would say any such thing.

"Alright, Meg." Director Merritt sighed. "Come along."

Meg didn't even look back at Miss Moroni. No doubt Miss Moroni was disappointed at Meg's good luck. Miss Moroni was so mean-spirited. Meg didn't even want to see it.

Director Merritt called for one of the Army mechanics and they climbed into the front seat of the Director's long black car. Meg sat in the back. She ran her fingers over the sharp edges of the envelope in her hand. The two men occupied themselves with discussing how best to make the repair. Meg was glad she didn't have to try to make conversation with them.

Meg hadn't been on the road down to Lone Pine since the Binnenkerks arrived in California. It wouldn't have changed much, but Meg realized it looked different to her. It looked different because it felt familiar. There was the tree she had seen on the way up. There was the white bleached lake. There was the abandoned gas station all by itself at the empty corner of two intersecting roads.

Then Meg could see the bus alongside the road. Director Merritt pulled over behind it.

"I'll thank you forever for this," Meg said to Director Merritt as she slipped out of the car.

"Now, don't rush, Meg," Director Merritt said. "Be careful along the road."

"I promise I'll find you in just a minute."

Meg ran alongside the bus, looking in the windows for Deanna. The older men had gotten off the bus to look into the engine, but the women stayed on the bus out of the dust. Meg spotted Deanna and her mother sitting side by side. Meg rapped on the glass window. Deanna looked over in surprise, then she immediately stood up and squeezed past her mother to make her way up the aisle and off the bus.

"Deanna!" Meg called and flew giddily toward her. "I can't believe I found you in time! I brought you a present."

Meg handed her the envelope. "Here. It's just a flower I pressed from when we went hiking. Up into the mountains. That day."

"Meg. I can't believe you made it here."

"I got a ride. Miss Moroni hates me, by the way."

"Who's Miss Moroni?"

"Exactly!" Meg laughed until she choked. Then she grabbed Deanna by both shoulders. "Listen, I know it won't take them long to fix the bus, but I want to make sure you know that you're my best friend, and you have to write to me as soon as you know your address, because I'm not going to lose you, and maybe I'll marry Frank and maybe I won't."

"What?" Deanna interjected.

"Or maybe I won't," Meg repeated, "but you're not going to lose him and you're not going to lose me, as long as you write and send me your address, got it?"

"Yes, Meg."

"We'll still be in Independence for a while, so I'll get your letter. See, I already put my address and a stamp on the envelope."

"You did?" Deanna laughed.

"Yes, so no excuses, and you can even write to me in Japanese but remember I never learned much kanji."

"I know less kanji than you do. We will definitely be writing in English."

"Good. Okay." Meg politely waved to Mrs. Matsumoto on the bus. "Thank you for letting Deanna be friends with me," she called.

Meg grabbed Deanna again and hugged her. It struck Meg that she had never in her entire life grabbed and hugged anyone before. But here, thanks to Mr. Evans and Director Merritt, she got that opportunity.

"Well, I better get back to Director Merritt."

"Director Merritt?"

"Yeah, he gave me a ride."

"You're kidding."

"I am not kidding."

"Maybe he should've driven us to the train station so we wouldn't have to deal with this bus."

"I don't think he was that eager to get rid of you," Meg smiled back.

"I'm going to miss you, Meg."

"We'll see each other again," Meg said. "But it might be a while. So you have to ...."

"I know. Write," Deanna said. "I will."

"Okay." Unsure what else to say, Meg looked off to the side and saw Director Merritt standing close by.

"Bye, Deanna," Meg said with a final squeeze all the way around her friend. Then she let go and walked over to Director Merritt.

The men stepped away from the bus engine. Before getting back on the bus, the older Japanese gentlemen came up to Director Merritt one by one, shook his hand, and bowed. Director Merritt had been their jailor, yet they were thanking him and showing him respect. Was there such a thing as an honorable jailor? If there was, Director Merritt had been one. The bus engine started up, new belt holding, and drove away, leaving Meg, Director Merritt and the Army mechanic in the dust by the side of the road.


## *The Rocks*


December during wartime was still December, after all, and that made it a month for giving and receiving gifts. That December of 1944, Germany decided to send a gift to Japan: a thousand pounds of what they labeled "U-powder," hoping Japan could succeed in making a bomb where they had failed. It was uranium oxide, not enriched, not separated. By the time the German submarine slipped out of the dock five months later with this precious cargo, the Americans had uncovered the plot and intercepted the submarine. The last ditch German attempt at a nuclear bomb failed.

Unfortunately, another gift did exchange hands in December of 1944. This one the Americans failed to intercept. A Los Alamos scientist met up with a Russian spy in Albuquerque, New Mexico, and handed over secrets to the bomb. Then the traitor returned to work as if nothing had happened.

General Groves foresaw that Russia would be the next significant adversary after the war, and he was right, but what he didn't know was that America's nuclear secrets had already been leaked. General Groves had worked tirelessly for a future in which the U.S. would be the world's sole atomic superpower. That plan unraveled before the bomb was even done.

Up in Los Alamos that December of 1944, Dr. Rotblat wrestled with his conscience. He knew that at the rate enriched U235 was being produced in Tennessee and plutonium was being produced in Washington, it would be months before the scientists received a critical mass of either. It was looking more and more likely that Germany would lose the war before America had a nuclear bomb.

Dr. Rotblat was tremendously grateful the Nazis were losing, but that meant a couple of things from his perspective. First, it meant nothing he was doing in Los Alamos would contribute to the liberation of Poland. Poland would be free from Nazi rule without a nuclear bomb. Second, it meant he could stop working on the bomb project altogether if he chose to. All his work would do was help push the world into a future that had nuclear bombs in it. He could stop.

Dr. Rotblat turned in his notice to General Groves and bought a ticket back to England. There, he awaited the end of the war, praying he hadn't lost his whole family in the Warsaw Ghetto.

In the wake of his departure, December of 1944 saw a tremendous accomplishment in Los Alamos. After months of meticulous tinkering, Los Alamos engineers got implosion explosives to work. A plutonium bomb could be ignited by a spherical patchwork of explosive lenses, linked and set to go off at precisely the same instant. With that obstacle overcome, a plutonium bomb finally became a viable alternative to the U235 bomb. General Groves was going to get both.

Meg Binnenkerk didn't know about any of these momentous developments, but there was one gift in December of 1944 that was announced for everyone to hear. That gift came from the United States Supreme Court. The Court agreed to hear a writ of habeas corpus filed by a young woman, Mitsuye Endo, who was being held in the Tule Lake War Relocation Center. Ms. Endo claimed that, as a loyal American, the government had no basis under the Constitution to lock her up. The government attempted to derail her case, first by moving her to a camp outside of California in an attempt to deprive the California court of jurisdiction, and then by offering to release her and her family so long as she agreed never to return to California. Ms. Endo said no. She held out to hear what the Supreme Court would say.

In December of 1944, the United States Supreme Court agreed with Ms. Endo, ruling that the government had no authority to continue to hold her in a prison camp and no authority to tell her where she could and could not relocate just because of her Japanese ancestry. Whatever the justification had been for the camps at the beginning of the war, the Supreme Court said that the

Constitution would not tolerate keeping admittedly loyal Japanese-Americans in custody any longer.

All of the folks saying no that month - saying no to letting Germany share secrets with Japan, or to keeping American secrets from Russia, or to continuing to work in Los Alamos, or to incarcerating Japanese-Americans -   they all thought saying no was one step toward setting things right.

Admittedly, there was one person who was less generous of spirit that December. That month, the Norwegian Nobel Committee announced the year's Nobel prize for Chemistry would go to German scientist Dr. Otto Hahn for the discovery of fission. Did Dr. Hahn use his acceptance speech to credit Dr. Ida Noddack, who'd described the phenomenon of fission four years before him, in reports he had called "absurd"? No, he didn't. In fact, he mocked her in a footnote in the published version of his Nobel lecture.

Did Dr. Hahn insist on sharing the Nobel prize with Dr. Lise Meitner, his mentor and long-time laboratory partner, who correctly explained the phenomenon and gave it the name "fission?" Nope, he didn't do that either. Dr. Hahn took the prize for himself alone.

Up in Washington State, Dr. Fermi and Dr. Marshall celebrated Christmas Day, 1944, by pushing the first irradiated slugs of uranium 238 from their giant reactor into a deep pool of chilled river water. The slugs would need time to cool. Then they would give up the most precious man-made element of all time: plutonium.

# Chapter 22
# A Rocky Ending

*Meg*

Each Sunday's church bulletin included a new list of names. Residents of Manzanar, family by family, were finding places to live outside the camp.

Every Sunday, Father and the other ministers wrote sentences of inspiration, encouraging the families to leave Manzanar with optimism rather than bitterness.

Father was restless. Maybe it was because his camp congregation was shrinking, week by week. Maybe he had contracted wanderlust from Mr. Adams. The photographer seemed so free, traveling around the west with his camera equipment.

"It's time to start talking about our next step," Father said to Mother one evening after supper. Meg and Walter were washing and drying the dishes together, but the kitchen was only steps away from the living room. Meg turned the spigot off at the sink so they both could hear clearly. Walter picked up the next dish and wiped it silently.

"Has your assignment ended?" Mother asked softly.

"The timing of a move is up to us. The more families move out of Manzanar, the less the need is for me here. And it may take a while to receive a call from a church. It's probably best to start putting out some inquiries now."

"Parish ministry, then?" Mother asked.

"I can't get back to Japan until the war is over, so, yes, either a church or teaching. A church position would be better, so I wouldn't need to wait until the end of a term or school year if I get a call back to Japan. I could leave without notice."

Mother fell silent. Walter looked up at Meg. They both realized Father had said "I could leave," not "we could leave." He was aiming to go back to Japan without them.

Finally Mother spoke. "We should go back to Zeeland, or at least somewhere in Michigan."

"It would be better to be closer to New York or D.C. so I can meet more often with the Mission Board."

"Howard," Mother said, and her voice dropped, but Meg and Walter could still hear her. "If you're going back to Japan, it would be better for me, and the children, to be near family. Rather than dropping us off somewhere where we don't know anyone."

"I'll have to go where I'm called," Father reminded her.

"Maybe you're called to be with your family," Mother said in the quietest voice Meg had ever heard, a voice like a faint crack of ice far out on a pond, like the zipper on a body bag.

Meg and Walter looked at each other and acknowledged silently this was no longer a conversation for them to hear. Meg tiptoed back to her bedroom. Water slipped out the back door.

It turned out neither Father's wish to be near Washington D.C. or New York, nor Mother's wish to return to Michigan, was granted.

"Albuquerque!?" Mother exclaimed.

"There's a large Presbyterian church there where I can serve as an associate minister," Father said. "I can stay as long as the war lasts. And then we'll see."

"I don't know a single thing about Albuquerque."

"We traveled through it on the train to get here."

"Yes, but we never got off the train."

"When have we ever gotten an advance look at our next assignment?"

"I'll consider it," Mother said, in that new soft, dangerous tone.

The next day, Mother had made up her mind. She made her announcement at the supper table, in full earshot of the children.

"I have come to a decision."

Father looked up from his plate at Mother.

Mother continued. "We will go to Albuquerque, but only if there is a position for me as well."

Father seemed speechless.

Mother repeated herself. "I will only go to Albuquerque, and take these children with me, if there's a post for me at the church as pianist or organist."

"And if there isn't?" Father asked.

"Then we stay here until you get a call that invites both of us."

Mother picked up the bowl of potatoes and passed it, as if nothing momentous had just happened, as if they hadn't already eaten their fill of potatoes.

Mother sighed. "When we went off to Japan, it was together. I came back alone because I had no choice.

When we came here, again there was no choice. But now we have a choice. And I won't be dragged from pillar to post just because of the winds of war."

Mother trembled, then delivered her final statement. "This is a decision we will make together."

Father looked around the bare little house, perpetually dusty from the Owens Valley winds. Perhaps he saw it for the first time, the dwelling to which he'd brought his family during wartime so that he could minister to the incarcerated Japanese-Americans.

"Alright, Esther. I'll inquire whether there's a need for a pianist or organist at the church in Albuquerque."

"Excuse me." Mother slid her chair back and took the few steps into the back bedroom. Just then, Amy threw her spoon across the room with a swing of her arm, knocking over her milk cup. Meg reached for the cup, righted it on the table outside of Amy's reach, and then went to the kitchen for a wash rag.

Maybe it would be Albuquerque. Maybe it wouldn't. It didn't really matter to Meg. She felt in her sweater pocket the letter she had received from Deanna, still in the envelope where Deanna had printed her return address. Meg didn't care where she was going, because wherever the Binnenkerks landed, she would send

Deanna her new mailing address. Meg felt the paper in her pocket and knew that, as long as she protected that envelope, somewhere out there in the crazy world, she had a friend.

## *The Rocks*

As the Binnenkerks prepared to move to Albuquerque, pilots stationed at Albuquerque's Kirtland Army Air Field began to prepare for their new mission. They would be flying B-29 bombers modified to carry American nuclear weapons fueled by Africa's fiercest rocks across the sea, not to Germany, but to Japan.

If it weren't for the rocks in the bed,
the stream would have no song.

Carl Perkins